Slightly Spooky Stories IV

Patsy Collins

Contents

1. Dream Wedding

Immediately Briony woke, she knew she'd been having that dream again. The one in an imposing and unfamiliar church, not the cosy wood-panelled registry office which would be the real venue. Her dress wasn't right either. The floral one with the matching jacket she'd selected for her big day was a far more sensible choice than the gorgeous cascade of white lace from her dream.

"If anyone knows why this man should not be joined to this woman in holy matrimony, speak now or forever hold thy peace," the vicar had said.

"I do," a woman's voice had called from the back, as it always did at that point in her dream. "I, Mary Valerie Louisa Stuart, know this wedding must not take place."

As usual that's when Briony had woken up. Something had been different this time, though Briony couldn't think what. It couldn't really matter. All brides got pre-wedding nerves, didn't they? Even her friend Stella had admitted having a dream where she broke the heel of her shoe, the best man lost the rings and the groom's mother couldn't stop sneezing. She'd not said so straight away though.

"Maybe it's a sign you shouldn't be marrying Carter?" had been her initial reaction.

"Don't start that again," Briony had retorted.

"I haven't started anything. It was you who asked what the

dream meant, and that's an obvious way to interpret it."

"Yeah, like the way it was obvious to assume Carter was only interested in my compensation money."

"I didn't say that was all he was interested in! Just that, as you met him right after the settlement for your leg was announced in the paper, you should consider the possibility and not rush into marriage until you knew him better."

Briony knew that was both true, and sensible advice. Carter had proved such caution wasn't needed by readily agreeing to a pre-nup guaranteeing she'd keep her money if they divorced within five years. He'd not minded that they delay the wedding either, although he'd made the wrong assumption about that.

"Briony wants to wait until her leg is strong enough for her to stand throughout the ceremony," he told people.

She'd gone along with that, rather than confess to doubting him, as she no longer did.

Stella had taken more convincing, as Briony reminded her. "You thought he didn't talk about his years in Australia because he had something to hide."

"I didn't know about his first wife then, did I?" Stella had defended herself.

Emily had died in Carter's arms, just a few weeks after their wedding. He'd blamed himself.

"We'd gone for a picnic so she could show me the outback," he told Briony. "She tripped and banged her head. At first she seemed OK, but she got sleepy and we stopped to rest… She didn't wake up." Tears had run down his face. "Concussion, the doctors said. I should have realised she wasn't well, should have turned back."

He'd admitted the long distance they'd driven to the start

of their walk, and remoteness of the location, meant that however soon he'd tried to get help it would still have been too late. That didn't stop him feeling responsible. "She'd said there was nothing there but dust and rocks, but knew it was my wish to go walkabout and wanted all my wishes to come true."

Was it any wonder he didn't want to discuss his time in Australia? Briony felt haunted by the memory herself; the woman in her dreams was usually called Emily…

Briony rang her friend. "You know my dream? I've just realised it's not always exactly the same."

"Not always?" Stella asked. "How often do you have it?"

"Most nights," Briony admitted. "It's starting to worry me and, as it keeps waking me, I'm getting so tired."

Stella had insisted they meet for coffee and that Briony tell her as much about the dreams as she could recall.

"It sounds very old-fashioned," Stella remarked. "Do vicars still say the 'hold thy peace' bit?"

"I don't know. It's not like that in the service we're having, but the registrar said they can't use the same wording as for religious weddings."

Stella then asked when the dreams started.

"The first time was just before I got you to come to the bridal shop with me. Do you remember?"

"How could I forget? All those frills and lace were totally out of character."

"They were beautiful …"

"Sure, but totally not your kind of thing. The flowery dress is lovely, much more you, and something you can wear again."

"You're right. I don't know what I was thinking."

"Maybe looking for the dress from your dream? Subconsciously trying to make sense of it?"

"Perhaps."

"Is it just the woman's name which changes?"

"No, it's actually a different woman. Or women. It's hard to remember. I'm pretty sure everything else is the same, but it's not always Emily who speaks."

"Emily? Carter's first wife?"

"I guess so. It makes sense that, if I'm to have an anxiety dream about the wedding, she would be there. Oh! I suppose I could find out her surname."

"Easily – just ask Carter."

"He gets upset if I mention her, but it'll be on the wedding paperwork somewhere, won't it?"

"Maybe. But, even if it is, how does that help?"

"The women always give their full names. Pretty sure Emily Olivia Dickinson is what she said."

"And the woman last night?"

"Mary, something, something Stuart. It half rang a bell, but I don't know anyone called that. There was another Mary too, I think."

"Keep a notebook by your bed and write them down, I've got a theory."

Briony did as instructed over the next couple of nights and reported back to her friend. "I've worked it out! It was Mary Anning who put me on the right track. She was a famous fossil hunter from Lyme Regis – which is where Carter is taking me on honeymoon. I'd read about her searching among the rocks for Troglodytes or whatever they're called."

"Trilobites?" Stella suggested.

"Could be. Anyway, it sounded like fun – and it'll be romantic walking along the beach, won't it?"

"Hmmm. Carter gave you the book did he?"

"Yes. Just shows how well he knows me. Normally I wouldn't even look at that sort of thing, but this was a story, not a text book, and it was really good."

"OK, so that explains why Mary Anning was in your dream, and Emily makes sense, but what about the other Mary?"

"If you take out the middle names you have Mary Stuart – who was Mary Queen of Scots."

"Yes." Stella didn't sound surprised.

"Oh, was that your theory? They're just famous names I've heard?"

"I did wonder. Emily Dickinson is a famous poet. Was Dickinson the maiden name of Carter's first wife?"

"Don't know. I've been trying to find out, but it's difficult without telling him I've been dreaming she's trying to stop us getting married. I don't think I should say that, do you?"

"I suppose not, but keep trying to find out."

"Will do, and I'm going to see what else I can find out about those women."

"You're going to end up knowing all sorts of random stuff. We should start doing pub quizzes."

Briony laughed. "I'm not sure you get long enough to dream the answers."

She wasn't laughing a few days later when she found Emily and Carter's wedding certificate and learned his first wife really was named Emily Olivia Dickinson, just like the woman in her dream. At first Briony was troubled simply because she'd been snooping through Carter's things when he'd nipped out to fetch fresh croissants for their breakfast after she'd spent a night at his place. He'd almost caught her putting the file of papers back in the drawer.

Later she did an internet search and learned Emily Dickinson the poet had Elizabeth, not Olivia, as her middle name. Another search revealed that Mary Stuart, Queen of the Scots, didn't have the middle names given in the dream and neither did novelist Mary Stewart. Briony hadn't just dreamed about famous people she'd heard of, there was more to it than that. Briony couldn't shake the feeling the full names had some meaning, and that she wouldn't end the cycle of bad dreams and poor sleep until she found the answer. She kept searching until…

"Is your leg hurting?" Carter asked. "You're very pale."

"It's a bit stiff. I think I'll go for a walk, see if that helps."

"I'll get our coats."

"No!" She'd spoken more sharply than she intended. "The football is just about to start. I'd feel bad if you missed it."

"That's sweet of you, but give me a call if you get tired and I'll come and pick you up. Promise me?"

She couldn't get through to Stella at first, as she was on another call. When her friend answered she said, "I've got the kettle on."

"Ha! You must have known I was on the way!"

"I did. Carter just told me. He said your leg was hurting…"

"It isn't," Briony interrupted.

"…but that you'd say it isn't because you don't like making

a fuss. You're right, he does know you much better than I thought."

"Better than I know him anyway. Do me a favour and look up Mary Valerie Louise Stuart and head injury. I'll be there in a minute."

As soon as Briony arrived she demanded, "Did you find anything?"

"Yeah. A woman of that name died of a head injury," Stella said.

"A quite well off woman, who'd not been married long?"

Stella tapped away on her lap top. "Yes. So?"

"I found the same, then I researched Emily's death. It was concussion just like Carter said, but it seems there was some doubt it was an accident. According to friends she hated the outback with its heat, dust and deadly insects – it was one of the reasons she was so keen to marry a penniless Englishman and come here to live."

"Friends are often suspicious. You know what I was like when you first got engaged. Besides, you said Carter blames himself for the accident, because she went there for him. And he's not exactly penniless."

"Not now, because he got her money. She wasn't mega rich, but she'd inherited a house and some cash not long before they met… And he kept telling her friends how the heat made her feel faint, just like he tells people my leg still gives me problems."

"It does."

"Not as much as he says and, I didn't tell you before, but when I had a bad dream at his place he let slip that Emily had them too. He covered it by saying all brides did and you backed that up, but I wonder if she'd had the same warning as me."

"That's why you dream about the old fashioned dress and everything – it's Mary Stuart's wedding you see?"

"I think so."

"What about Mary Anning? She didn't die of a head injury, did she?" Stella asked.

"No, but because of the book Carter gave me about her, I'm going to spend my honeymoon somewhere that'll be pretty deserted at this time of year, and where there are slippery rocks. No one will be surprised if I fall and bang my head."

"Oh my God! He put the idea to go there into your head, and tried to make it so I'd back him about you having a little trouble walking, but being too stubborn to take it easy."

"What can I do? I don't have any evidence and if I tell the police about the dreams they'll think I'm crazy."

"Maybe, but if you tell them they'll have a record in case anything happens and we could put something on the internet about your weird dreams and what we've found out, to warn anyone else Carter might try this with. First though, call off the wedding."

Briony called Carter from Stella's landline, which she set to record the conversation. His response to the news she wasn't going to be marrying him and that she'd be reporting her suspicions to the police wasn't just angry, it was manic. As he ranted, Stella called the police who arrived promptly. They soon decided the recording should be shared with their colleagues in Australia as it was probably enough evidence to reopen the case into Emily's death.

Briony's dreams stopped after that – and she was sure she'd escaped a nightmare.

2. The Book Of Loss

The little red book appeared in Louise's bedroom, just like that. One moment it wasn't there and the next it was. Maybe it was magic or something?

No doubt her sister Claire would say it had been there absolutely ages and she'd just not seen it because she never, ever tidied up. Claire was annoying like that. Actually she was annoying in a lot of ways, but criticising Louise and exaggerating were high on the list. As were being boring, and spoiling Louise's fun every chance she got.

Louise picked up the book, vowing that if there was anything special about it, she wasn't going to tell Claire. It was old looking and scruffy. The gold letters of the title were flaking off the red leather binding, but Louise could just make out it was called The Book Of Loss. That didn't sound like a fun read. Flicking through the pages she was even more disappointed. There were no love potions, or spells to instantly become famous, not even a tip for turning your sister into a toad.

Other than right at the beginning the pages held no printing. Instead people had written in it and then in most cases apparently rubbed out their words again. Louise turned back to the beginning. The ink was faded and every s appeared as an f, so it took a while to work it out.

Instructions for use.

Write that which you wish to lose and erase the same. It will be gone from the world as it is from the page.

Beware! Take Care! That which is done cannot be undone.

Wow! If this thing worked she could remove every annoyance from her life. From the world. She'd get rid of homework, her excess weight, next door's yappy little dog. Why stop there? She could end wars and hunger and illness. She'd be a hero. A goddess sort of.

"Louise! Come on, tea's ready!" Claire yelled. It wasn't the first time either, but she didn't see why she should jump every time Claire told her to do something. She might act like it, but she wasn't her mum.

Those warnings in the book reminded her of Claire's nagging. Well, despite what her big sister said, she wasn't a complete idiot. She'd test it out first. 'Exam worries' she wrote and then erased. Perfect. She chucked the book back onto the pile of dirty laundry, overdue library books and things she'd borrowed from her sister and went down to see what Claire had cooked.

For once Mum was back from work on time, but that didn't stop Claire having a go.

"I hope you were revising?"

"Chill," Louise said. "It's only my mocks, not the real thing." Of course that was true, but Louise hadn't realised it before. In fact she'd been really worried about getting poor grades. Probably due to Claire going on about them all the time.

With typical double standards, when Louise said she was going back up to her room to revise, Claire said, "Do the washing up first. I've got a date and Mum deserves to put her feet up for a bit."

Once back in her room, Louise wrote 'Claire', 'a stone and a half' and 'next door's yappy dog' in her book. She didn't rub them out though – she'd only made Claire's name a little fainter before she dropped her eraser. It bounced off somewhere and she couldn't find it.

At school the next day, Louise asked about some of the words she'd seen in The Book Of Loss which hadn't been erased. Rationing and War were the ones she was particularly puzzled about. Why would anyone decide they should be kept?

"Sir, why was there food rationing?" she asked in history class.

"That's a little off topic, but as you're interested… By only allowing people a small amount of certain foods, it meant that everybody could have some. Without rationing, it wouldn't be divided fairly and prices would rise so high that many might starve."

"And it happened because of war?"

"That's right. Imports were reduced and production was down, because so many people were away fighting. Now, shall we get back to the Civil War?"

As the lesson continued Louise realised that ending war might bring more problems as well as solving them. Louise needed to be careful what she wrote in the little red book. With a fresh eraser she rubbed out just the word 'yappy' and the 'a' from her weight loss aims. She didn't really want to kill a dog and losing a lot of weight all at once could be dangerous.

It was oddly quiet. Next door's dog wasn't yapping and Claire wasn't yelling for her to get herself downstairs.

Eventually Louise went down of her own accord.

Tea was just salad. "Sorry, I was going to do chips, but I didn't have time," Claire said. She looked exhausted.

Julie, worried she'd weakened her by starting to erase her name in the book said, "That's OK, I want to cut down a bit anyway."

"Really? You can count on me to help."

Up until then Claire had never mentioned Louise's weight, but from then on she became the diet police. No crisps or chocolate made their way into Louise's lunchbox, no chips or pizza were found on her plate at teatime and she got lumbered with walking next door's dog. It had stopped yapping so much because Claire had been taking it on long walks, which also explained her sister's tiredness.

By the time Louise got her disastrous mock exam results, she was convinced the book had no magical properties. She'd occasionally dabbed at Claire's name when her big sister had been particularly annoying, but she was still there. Actually she was present more than ever, as these days she rarely went out unless she had to. Louise had been erasing a letter a week from 'a stone and a half'. Her weight had steadily dropped, but that was through diet and exercise. Next door's dog was always quiet now. When bringing it in from a walk one day, Louise had noticed it's reaction the the French doors. Stupid thing had been arguing with its own reflection. Once its owner realised, she kept the blind closed and the yapping stopped for good. Of course Louise didn't get any praise when she got things right, just complaints when she didn't.

Claire gave her a right lecture. "How many times did I tell you to revise?" she'd demanded. "I offered to help, but you said it was all OK."

"It is. Chill will you? I'm not worried, so why should you be?"

"Because it's your future, and because Mum…"

Louise didn't listen to the rest, because she was heading for her room. She grabbed The Book Of Loss and swiped the eraser over Claire's name. Just once, then she looked at the space where 'Exam worries' had been written. Not having the stress had been a relief, but her total lack of concern meant she'd put in no effort at all. That had been a mistake. Thankfully her teachers had been sympathetic and she'd be allowed another try at the end of term.

"I know things are difficult at home," more than one said.

They weren't though, not for Louise. Mum worked full time in the week as well as weekends and some evenings at the supermarket. As well as studying for her A levels Claire did most of the housework and tried to make up for Mum either being away or tired most of the time. She was doing it for Louise and wearing herself down in the process. Julie felt bad about adding to their burdens by rarely doing chores until nagged, performing poorly at school and being argumentative.

She went downstairs to apologise. Mum was back from work and sitting on the sofa, hugging Claire. For a moment Louise was pleased to see Mum looked the least tired of the two, but quickly realised it was only because Claire looked worse.

"What's wrong?"

Claire held out a hand to Louise, who took it and sat next to her sister.

"She's not well, love," Mum said.

"What's wrong?" She had been told Claire had anaemia.

That wasn't a big deal though. It just meant she wasn't getting enough iron and needed tablets and spinach.

Mum explained it wasn't that simple and Julie's body couldn't absorb enough iron. "She's started a treatment though and tomorrow she's going in to see if it's working."

Clearly neither of them thought it was and, looking at Claire, Louise could see why. Claire was so drained… as though being erased. She'd caused this! Maybe she could stop it? She had to try.

"I'll be back in a second." She raced upstairs and hunted for the red book. Claire was right, she really should keep her room a bit tidier. When she eventually found it, Louise wrote over Claire's name in bold strong letters, then went back down.

"I'm sure the treatment is working," she said as confidently as she could. "You were looking great this week, until you found out about my exam results. You're probably just upset over that."

"She could be right," Mum said. "You didn't look anything like as poorly this morning."

Louise made them all a cup of tea, explained that she could retake her exams and would work hard to pass this time. "And I'll try and help out a bit more at home."

No one was home when Louise got in from school the next day. Mum had texted to say they had a long wait at the hospital, so she wasn't surprised.

They would be though. Louise gathered all the laundry from her bedroom floor and shoved as much as she could in the washing machine. She put away the washing-up which had been draining since breakfast, and ironed her shirt for school the next day. Then she ironed Mum's work uniform.

And then everything else in the linen basket.

Mum sent another text. 'It's good news! Will explain when we get back – about an hour. Mum x'.

Louise put jacket potatoes and chicken portions in the oven. While it was cooking she collected everything else off her bedroom floor and chair and put them where they should be – including those items which belonged in Claire's wardrobe.

Soon The Book Of Loss was the only untidy thing in the room. She was tempted to write and erase problems for Mum and Claire, but she'd learned the dangers of that. Just having the book could be dangerous.

Louise made on final entry. She wrote 'The Book Of Loss' and the thoroughly erased it.

The little red book disappeared from Louise's bedroom, just like that. One moment it was there and the next it wasn't.

3. Mrs McEwan

I'd only been parked outside Mum's old house a few minutes and hadn't even had time to worry what had happened to Archie when I got a call from him.

"I'm fine," he assured me. "But I'm caught up in a crash on the motorway. My car is blocked in by others which were damaged and some poor devil is having to be cut out of his. I've got to give a statement too as I saw it happen."

"That's awful. Are you sure you're OK?"

"A bit shook up, I admit. It was the weirdest thing; I'll tell you about it later. I'm not hurt at all though and the car is fine. I'm sure I'll be be able to drive once I can actually leave, but I've no idea how long it will be before I get there. I'm so sorry."

"Don't worry about me. It'll be OK, just give me a really big hug when you get here, OK?"

"Will do. We'll both be needing that."

After the call I sat in the car, trying to nerve myself up to go in and look through the last of Mum's things. Might as well. Waiting outside knowing she wasn't inside to greet me and never would be, wasn't doing me any good at all. I'd not wanted to do this alone, but that didn't mean I couldn't. It wasn't as though I had to shift heavy furniture or anything like that. Archie and I didn't need any of it ourselves and it wouldn't suit our house anyway. Actually there wasn't anything in there we needed. All the important paperwork had been gathered up and dealt with right after her death. Before that, when Mum first got ill, she'd given away all the items of most value – financial and sentimental.

"I'd rather give them as presents and see people enjoy them, than for them to inherit them and associate them with my death," she'd said.

"That's a lovely idea."

"I thought of it when I was talking to Mrs McEwan one day. She was dropping hints about how much she liked my ruby brooch."

As if the memory had conjured her up, Mrs McEwan walked up the street towards me. Her hair, backlit by the sun, looked almost like a halo. At least, it would if haloes were crinkly like the tightest of perms and coloured a glowing lilac. I'm sure she was unaware of the effect. She's not someone who generally tries to stand out. She still wore a nondescript coat and old lady boots and she still carried a bulging string bag.

I pushed the button to open my window and called out a greeting.

"Beth dear, how lovely to see you!" she responded. "Hasn't the house been sold?"

"It has, and a clearance company are going to take all the furniture and things. I just wanted to look round one last time and see if there was anything else I wanted to keep."

She didn't remark on the fact I was still in my car, not in the house. Instead she gestured to the supermarket bag on the passenger seat. "Do you have any milk in there?

"Yes."

"To make tea?"

"Yes. Oh! Would you like a cup?"

"That would be lovely."

We went into the house together. Me glad of her company, her possibly actually wanting tea. Most likely not though. On the surface it often seemed as though it was her being helped, but there was often more to it than that. The first time Mum met her, Mrs McEwan's string bag came apart and Mum had helped her gather up a huge number of oranges. Another time I'd been about to go on a date, when I'd had to help her up after a fall.

Mum hadn't been happy about me going out with that boy. She'd reluctantly agreed though, provided I never went on his motorbike. I had promised I wouldn't. He'd come to the house on foot, but had his bike just around the corner. I should have been concerned that he'd been willing to trick her and make me break my promise, but I was too infatuated to say no when he handed me the crash helmet.

I'd been about to put it on when I heard a cry.

"What was that?"

"I didn't hear anything," the boy said.

"Beth dear, is that you? I've fallen and …"

"Stay still, I'm coming!"

"Oi! Where are you going?" my date demanded.

"That old lady is a friend of Mum's and I'm going to help her."

He didn't come with me. I got Mrs McEwan on her feet and she declared she was fine. "I heard a crack and thought it was my hip, but I must have landed on this stick."

The boy wasn't waiting when I got back to where he'd parked his bike. That was a good thing, as it saved me dumping him. Breaking the rules was one thing, failing to help someone in need was quite another.

When I'd met my Archie I hadn't been that taken with him at first, but I happened to bump into Mrs McEwan right after I'd turned him down. It suddenly occurred to me that if he'd been there when she fell, he wouldn't just have helped her up, but would have insisted on seeing her home – something which hadn't occurred to me. The next time he asked me out I accepted. Our love was the slow burn kind and the flame still warms me all these years later.

We invited her to our wedding. The whole thing was such a blur that I'm not sure I'd have realised Mrs McEwan had come if she hadn't been standing outside the church when Mum and I arrived. Mum was giving me away of course, so it was just us in the taxi.

"I'm so glad she's here," Mum said. "I'd have asked you to invite her if you hadn't thought of it yourself."

It wasn't until Mum had only a few days left that I learned why she'd felt so strongly about that.

"Remember I told you about the first time I met Mrs McEwan?"

"She dropped a lot of oranges you said. Was she going to make marmalade, do you think?"

"That's what I guessed at the time, but… Beth love, I'd just discovered I was pregnant with you. Forgive me, but I thought it was a disaster."

I'd squeezed Mum's hand. "It's OK. I always knew I wasn't planned and it can't have been easy for you."

"It was! Oh it was hard work at times, and we had nothing to start with, but you've always brought me the greatest joy since the first time I held you."

Knowing how I felt about my own kids I believed her.

"It would have been a tragedy to miss out on all that."

"Were you thinking of having me adopted?" I'd guessed.

"No, I was in too much of a state to think at all. I was walking beside the river, wanting all my problems to be over. Right by the weir it was. A dangerous spot."

"You were going to jump?"

"I didn't want to, and I didn't want to hurt you, but… Your father had moved on and I had no way to contact him. I was sure my parents would kick me out and I had no money. Just for a moment it seemed I had no hope and slipping into the water was my only option."

"And Mrs McEwan stopped you?"

"In a way. I saw her walking along and felt I had to wait until she was out of sight. She nearly was when her bag burst. I think that even by then I had begun to come to my senses. When I collected her oranges she put them back in the bag which was still broken and they spilled out again. I told her it was hopeless, but she said nothing ever was quite as bad as it seemed. She was right. Between us we managed to knot the bag up so the oranges stayed in, and I didn't do such a bad job raising you."

"You are a wonderful mum." She still was at that point, but I lost her soon after.

Chatting to Mrs McEwan as I sorted through Mum's things helped a lot. I did shed some tears, but I laughed too. In the end I decided not to take anything else away. The people who were doing the clearance worked for a charity, so I knew anything left behind would be used or sold to help people in need.

"Mum's already given me some keepsakes. I don't need more than those and my memories," I told Mrs McEwan.

"Talking of which, she wanted you to have this." I held out the ruby brooch she'd told Mum she admired.

"That's lovely of her, but I can't take it."

"You can. You've done so much for us and…"

"No, Beth I really can't. And now I must go."

I was still waving her off when I got a text from Archie. "Put the kettle on, I'm almost there!"

I did as he asked and then I tipped away the full mug Mrs McEwan had left behind. As I'd suspected she hadn't wanted a drink at all – only wanted to help me, just as she always has.

Archie pulled me into the big hug we'd promised each other.

"You really are OK?" I asked.

"I am, but I feel bad about leaving you to deal with all this on your own."

"Actually I didn't have to. Mrs McEwan was here."

He seemed really puzzled, but then he doesn't know that much about her. There's so much I could have told him, but somehow when she's not actually with me, I tend to forget about her. She just fades from my memory.

"She's the old lady who saved me and Mum before I was born," I prompted.

"That's who I was thinking of. It's so weird, but I thought I saw her today."

"That's not weird. She left here just before you arrived. You probably drove past her."

"I've never seen her before, remember?"

"Oh, that's right… but I've described her. Not all that many old ladies have lilac hair or still use those old string bags."

"True. Perhaps that explains why I was so sure it was her, but… It's strange I just felt that I absolutely knew it was Mrs McEwan. Anyway, it wasn't on this road I saw her. It was on the motorway right before the crash. She was in the back of a car which overtook me and the shock of recognising her made me lift my foot off the accelerator for a moment. If I hadn't…"

"OK, that is a bit weird. It can't have really been her though. If she was right in front of you, she'd have been caught up in the crash too and she's been with me all afternoon."

"How can she have been here, love?"

"She just walked up the path, carrying that string bag of hers."

"Like she did sixty-three years ago?"

"Yes… Oh!" Mum was only in her twenties when I was born, so someone she described as old might not have been any more ancient than I am now. Even so, that made Mrs McEwan over a hundred and twenty. I remembered the untasted tea, the fact that until today only Mum and I seemed to see her and that she didn't show in any of mine and Archie's wedding photos. "She can't really have been here, can she?"

"No. Perhaps she never was?"

"Maybe not," I admitted, but I knew she'd be back if I ever needed her again.

4. Book Of Dreams

Misha found the battered green book in her bag after a careers day at school. 'Put Yourself In The Picture' it said on the front. It sounded like a child's game, one she'd have loved when she was younger. Who was she kidding? She still loved sketching people and making up stuff about them.

That was Misha's dream, to be an artist of sorts. Not the kind who created accurate landscapes; cameras could do it better. Not a portrait painter flattering his subjects; she wanted her work to tell the truth. Not a surrealist or modern artist; she wanted the viewer to understand what they were looking at. And not someone all pretentious and 'look at me'. It was her drawings she wanted to get the attention and for them to make people happy. Since she was little she'd drawn things to try to help others. When a classmate lost a brother she'd drawn them both together to show he was still with her in a way. When Mum couldn't afford the house anymore she'd drawn them all in the new flat, to show that was home now and they could be happy there. If friends were scared of the dentist, or embarrassed about sticky out ears, she'd drawn something to make them feel better.

What Misha did wasn't a waste of time exactly, but it wasn't a job.

"It won't feed you and put a roof over your head, love," Mum had pointed out.

Maybe that's why someone had put the green book in her bag? To remind her to give up kid's stuff and focus properly on her future?

Misha looked at it properly. It was actually a tiny sketchbook, not a game. About thee-quarters of the pages have been drawn on, each one by a different person as far as she could tell. Some looked to be very old, as did the book itself. There were a couple of pages which might once have been printed with an introduction or instructions, but were now unreadable.

Some of the older sketches were too faint to make out properly. Some were difficult to fathom because they weren't very good. Some were obvious though, a wedding, a mother with a baby and a boy in front of a ship. There are people with money, and people with unidentifiable things. There was someone baking, another jumping and one who might be a Morris Dancer.

Only one picture was of someone Misha thought she recognised and then only because of the context. The drawing was clearly of the newspaper offices in town and the person in front of it was obviously a woman. Misha guessed she was the current editor. The paper had run a piece on the news from fifty years previously, mentioning that's when the editor first began working with them, and she'd been in to the school that day to talk about aiming high but being prepared to start at the bottom and work up to what you wanted.

Misha saw the drawing had a name and date. Stephanie Lawrence 1967. It really was of the newspaper editor then. There were several drawing after hers, so it might not have been her who gave the book to Misha, but maybe she'd know who did.

At lunchtime the next day, Misha ran down to the office and asked to see the editor.

"Do you have an appointment?"

"No, but can you tell her it's about a little green book."

To Misha's surprise, the editor asked her to go straight up. She asked to see the book and flicked through the last few drawings. "It's had some use since I saw it last."

"You didn't give it to me?" Misha asked.

"No, but I think I know why you have it. Tell me your hope, child."

Misha told her about wanting to be an artist. "But it's not something you can do as a job."

"What about Rembrandt, Cezanne, Van Gogh?"

"They all went mad or died in poverty!"

"Oh dear. But there are others. What kind of things do you paint?"

After Misha explained about her drawings, the editor said, "A cartoonist then! Thelwell, Shultz, Disney," they all did OK.

"And this book can make it happen?"

"I don't think so, not precisely, but it helps somehow. When I found it I recognised this picture." She turned to the mother and baby. "The lady was a neighbour and she'd just adopted a child. That was three years after the date on the picture."

"Maybe by drawing herself with a child she realised how much she wanted that and made sure it happened even if she couldn't have her own?" Misha suggested.

"Yes, I think it's something like that. All the pictures have names and dates. The boy with the ship joined the navy and became an admiral, luckily for me."

"Why for you?"

"Because that made him easy to research and as he'd lived locally I thought the paper might be interested so wrote about him. They didn't buy it, but were impressed with my enthusiasm and gave me a Saturday job. A girl working in a newspaper office wasn't unheard of back then, but it was unusual. Without that bit of luck I might never have achieved my dream."

"I think I understand," Misha said. "It didn't make it happen for you, but helped you do it for yourself."

Stephanie handed the book back to Misha. "When you've drawn in it, will you bring it back to show me?"

Misha promised that she would.

She was back a week later. In the book was a sketch of herself drawing. "But it's not that I really wanted you to see," she told Stephanie. "It's these." She handed over cartoons she'd made. There was one of Stephanie writing her own headline to celebrate her fifty years at the paper. At her feet where other newspapers, the headline of each being the most memorable events covered by the paper in her half century there.

"I love it!" Stephanie said. "Will you…"

"Please, look at the rest before you say anything."

Misha waited as the editor looked through her other cartoons. There was one of the local butcher saying his catchphrase, 'as tender as your first kiss' and the baker declaring 'everyone wants to get into my bloomers'. Another showed a tourist making a hash of saying local place names.

The last was of the local MP, whose party and his own voting had led to the closure of a local primary school. One which he'd previously visited at Christmas and given a patronising speech about children being the future. Misha had drawn him as Santa, with the children lined up to give him presents.

"These are all your own work?" Stephanie asked.

"Yes."

"And you did them since I saw you last?"

"Yes."

"Then I'd like you to become our cartoonist. We've never had one, and I'm afraid we can't pay much – but it will be enough for you to buy drawing materials and well…"

"It'll be a start. I can gain experience and get better and work my way up to doing it for a living?"

"Exactly."

Afterwards Misha was tempted to draw a picture of her mum looking happy and free from worries in the book, but she didn't think it would work that way. Besides, it wasn't up to her to decide other people's futures. Instead she slipped the book into the pocket of George Reynolds. She had no idea what his dreams might be, but he was a really nice man and he'd taken Mum to the pictures last night.

5. Stepping Into The Present

Gill found the tickets when checking Amos's coat pocket ready to take more of his things to the charity shop. The tickets were for Solent Castle and valid for a year from the day they were bought – meaning that day was the very last opportunity to use them. They brought back memories both of a nice day out and promises she and Amos had made to each other. When he was first diagnosed, they'd agreed to enjoy whatever time they had left together. Going to the castle had been part of that. She'd also assured Amos she'd try to be happy… afterwards.

"I don't think I can, Amos," she said to the empty room they'd once shared. "Not without going back in time to when you were with me."

Could it be that he was with her, in a way? Was that why she'd found the tickets when there was still time to use hers, but no time to think the matter over?

"What I promised was that I'd try, and that I can do." Gill left the sorting of clothes and drove herself to the castle.

Of course it brought back memories of Amos, but then everything did, and those from Solent Castle were happy ones. They'd enjoyed it there, walking round in the sunshine and sitting on every bench to soak in the atmosphere and occasionally for Amos to get his breath back. A lovely lunch they'd had in the cafe, and later tea and cake. Despite being there all day they hadn't seen everything. That wasn't due just to their frequent breaks but because the castle was being used as a film location.

As well as being a good excuse to rest without Amos feeling he was holding her back, Gill had been delighted because everyone was dressed in tudor costume. That was her favourite historical period and she'd read lots of books and watched dozens of films and TV dramas set then.

"It's just like being in *Wolf Hall* or *The Other Boleyn Girl*," she'd said to Amos.

"And you're the prettiest lady at court, my love." Amos had removed an imaginary hat and given a theatrical bow. "I don't want to be Henry the Eighth though. I know I've put on a few pounds since retiring, but I'm not that fat."

"You can be my handsome lute player."

"Not if a lute is one of those long trumpet affairs. I don't have the puff for that."

"No, it's the thing that looks like a guitar with the top bit bent back."

"I can probably manage that."

"You'd look lovely in doublet and hose."

"Tights you mean?"

"You've always had nice legs."

"I'd best use them then, hadn't I? Where shall we go next?"

"Over there." Gill pointed to a sign saying, 'Step Back In Time'.

The long gallery, which was almost eerily quiet, contained a series of sturdy tables topped with a different large scale models. Each was accompanied by a large sign board. The models and signs were well illuminated with spotlights. The first exhibit featured a hill with a wooden building on it and a moat surrounding both the hill and quite a large area of land. This, they learned from the sign, was how the earliest castle on the site was believed to have looked.

As they walked on they saw further representations of the castle at key points in its history. It was interesting to see what changed each time and what stayed the same. Gill read the signs aloud and they searched for the details mentioned.

"We're going to be experts on all these technical terms," Amos said, delighting Gill with his positivity.

Gradually they realised they had the space to themselves.

"Maybe we shouldn't be in here?" Gill said.

"There's no work or filming going on. Besides if we weren't supposed to be here, the door would have been locked, wouldn't it?"

"That's true."

They continued until they reached a model of the castle as it had looked just before the, almost complete, four year renovation project. There was room in the building for further displays in years to come.

"I enjoyed that," Amos said. "Wouldn't mind a quick sit down now though. After that we can look for a good spot to watch more of the filming if you like?"

"I would, just for a little while. After that we'll be ready for a cup of tea I should think."

"And a cake!"

The space wasn't lit beyond where the models and signs finished so they'd groped about when looking for somewhere to sit. It didn't take long to find a window seat.

"Shame the window is bricked up. It would be nice to

have some light here," Gill remarked.

"I don't think there would be any. Isn't that the cafe behind there?"

Once he said that, Gill could smell the coffee and hear the rattle of crockery. She'd looked around for something of interest, so Amos didn't feel bad for making her sit in the dark, and found a sign on the wall, just to the left of where he was sitting. It was made of thick metal and very dusty. She wiped it with a tissue, so she could read the raised lettering.

"Oh, you don't think it's a film prop, do you?"

"If it was they wouldn't leave it somewhere anyone could damage it," Amos assured her. "It's probably left over from whatever display was here before. What does it say?"

Gill inspected it. "Looks like you're right. 'Step back in time!' it's got and underneath it goes 'Pass through here and enter any time period you wish'."

"No guesses for when you'd go back to given the chance," Amos said.

"You're wrong. I wouldn't go back. I'm far happier here in the present with you."

"And me with you. I'd make it last forever if I could." He'd reached for her hand and squeezed it.

"I know," she'd whispered. Then in a louder, brighter, voice had said, "Give me some change then."

"Change? Oh, money you mean?"

"Yes. There's a donation box set into the wall below the sign. Says it's so they can keep making it possible for people to step back in time. I'd like to think of this display always being here so others can enjoy it just like we have."

Amos had emptied his pockets and insisted she feed it all

into the little box. "Don't worry, I've got a note left that's big enough for our cake later on."

They'd had some other nice trips out after that, but each time Amos had needed to stop more often and been ready to go home a bit sooner.

Some parts of Solent Castle looked different on Gill's second visit. The restoration was complete and the actors and film props had, of course, gone. It was just as busy though. There were a lot more hand rails and signs. Gill guessed some were new and some had been temporarily removed, to make the castle look less like a modern tourist attraction during filming, and had now been replaced.

Gill first went to the areas which hadn't been open when she'd come with Amos. There was a delightful courtyard garden filled with all kinds of herbs and scented flowers. Amos would have loved telling her all the different names.

She climbed up the tallest tower and walked out onto the battlements. In a way it was good that hadn't been open last time. Amos wouldn't have been able to come up and she'd not have wanted to abandon him while she made the climb. He'd have felt bad at her missing the opportunity and not believed her excuse of not fancying it anyway.

The one other place which had previously been shut was the chapel. It was lovely. Quite plain really. There was a simple metal cross on a wooden altar, and whitewashed walls with stone details here and there. What made it special was the light streaming in through the stained glass, creating patterns on the walls and floor. It spilled across the altar making the cross sparkle with red, gold and purple. Gill was reminded of the boarded up window in the 'Step Back Through Time' exhibit. Of course she must go there. She had a feeling it would have been extended with a model of the castle as it was now the restoration had rebuilt some of the walls, redefined the once collapsed and boggy moat, and repaired the crenellations on the battlement. It would be lovely to look at the newest model and remember Amos making a contribution towards its cost.

The exhibit was just as Gill recalled it, even down to the absence of any other people, right until the very end. There she found the model she'd hoped to see – one of the castle newly restored. It was a good one and, even better, the sign thanked all the generous visitors whose donations had made both the restoration and the new display possible.

"That's you, Amos," Gill whispered. It felt as though he were very close.

She smelled the coffee and heard the sounds of people working in the busy cafe, but wasn't tempted to hurry there. She had something else to do first.

Gill easily found the window seat Amos had rested on, and the sign and donation box nearby. With the extra model and sign there was now more light, so she was able to see that the sign wasn't screwed directly into the wall as she'd assumed, but affixed to an arched doorway. She moved closer and read the old sign again. 'Step back in time! Pass through here and enter any time period you wish.'

"If only I could, Amos," she said. "I'd step back to when you were with me."

There was a metal latch and handle on the door. Amos would have said that if she shouldn't go through then it would be locked. It didn't look locked, or even as though it could be. She reached out and pressed the lever. The door swung open. That shouldn't have been possible, or if it was she should now be looking into the cafe, but she wasn't. There seemed to be another exhibit beyond, just like the one she'd just walked through. Puzzled, Gill stepped through the arch and into the space beyond.

A clang caused her to look back and see the door had swung shut. Gill took another step forward. In front of her was a model of the first castle built on the site, exactly as she'd seen just now, and a year ago. Everything was exactly the same. Except there was a huge difference between those two visit. The first time she'd not been alone… But neither was she now.

"Amos?"

He reached for her hand and squeezed it. "I've been waiting, my love."

6. Crossing The Bridge

Rebekah drove through the French countryside to keep a date she'd made almost a year previously. None of it seemed quite real, from the despair she'd felt that first time, to the feelings of hope which now surged through her. Everything had gone right for her since she'd met Etienne. She was practically a different person.

Her family had welcomed her back without even a murmured 'told you so'. She was earning her keep with translation work and had begun a training course to become a language teacher, just as she'd dreamed she would. Although she'd believed Etienne when he'd said she'd have to wait for love, she was less sure it would find her. That was OK, she thought she knew where to look for it.

The changes she found in France were greater even than those she'd gone through. She could hardly believe how much the place had altered. The little stone bridge had been replaced by an ugly metal one carrying a dual carriageway over the river. The village was now a crowded town. She couldn't find the cafe in which she and Etienne had drunk coffee and chatted, but in the area where she thought it must have been was a music shop.

Rebekah went in and asked the assistant if he knew of Etienne Dupont. If everything else had changed so much, perhaps his life too had moved dramatically onwards?

"Of course," she was informed in French. "We have all his work. Are you interested in original vinyl or songs remastered onto cd?"

That made no sense until she picked up a record and on the back of the sleeve saw a picture of a man looking very like her Etienne. He must have been a relation, but even that didn't really explain it. Rebekah bought a cd and took it out to her car to listen.

The first song was hauntingly beautiful. It was about a girl and a boy on a bridge. About loss and regret, despair and doubt, hopes and dreams. The information leaflet told her it had been written over sixty years before. How was that possible when it described her meeting with Etienne and was titled 'Rebekah'?

A year previously Rebekah had pulled onto the verge and stopped the car. She'd thought she might have trouble driving on the 'wrong' side of the road but, thanks to her sat-nav reminders and plenty of signs when she left the ferry, it had been fairly easy. It was her tears which made further progress impossible. She should have known going to France to escape her problems wouldn't work. You can't run away from yourself; that's what people said and they were right. You can't run away from heartbreak either. She'd given up her studies and her dreams for love. She'd wanted Rob more than those things and thought he felt the same way. He'd left her and she was left with nothing.

She got out of the car and looked around. Although the town where she'd booked a room for the next couple of nights was close by, she was in open countryside. Anonymous drivers rushed by. A car slowed up as it approached and she waved in a manner she hoped indicated she was fine and that they should continue their journey.

The help she probably needed wouldn't come from some well-meaning stranger's toolkit.

The sun was warm and the dry air carried a pleasant scent of herbs from the wild marjoram growing amongst the grass under her feet. Perhaps she should go for a walk until she was composed enough to drive? With luck the exercise would help her to sleep. Rebekah followed a river, thinking that would ensure she didn't get lost.

But why care about getting physically lost when emotionally she was so adrift from any chance of happiness? The river could solve that problem for her. Rebekah could just allow herself to slide into the cool water. No one would know it wasn't an accident. No one would care anyway.

Just as Rebekah was beginning to feel uncomfortably warm, the riverside path took her into a wooded area. Lush ferns grew in the dappled shade and the sound of traffic was replaced by birdsong. It was peaceful, almost other worldly. The beauty and quiet soothed her and stopped desperately unhappy thoughts whirling through her mind.

For a time the path veered away from the river. Rebekah's next sighting of it included a pretty stone bridge carrying an empty road from one bank to the other. She must have walked further than she'd realised or in a very different direction as surely the main road should be nearby. There was no sight nor sound of it.

The only signs of life were a heavy looking traditional bicycle and a man sitting on the stone wall, cradling something in his arms and looking down into the deep water. What could he be doing? He didn't react to her approach, just shuffled himself a little further forward. If he wasn't careful he'd end up falling in. Then she saw he was holding a rock.

"Stop! Wait!" She repeated the words in French.

He did look up then. Thankfully he didn't jump before she reached him.

"Wait, please. Let me try to help." Again she spoke in French.

He shrugged, then swung one leg back over the wall so he was no longer so precariously balanced.

"Were you…?" She trailed off, not sure if asking him if he'd intended to end his life would help.

He shrugged again, but as he placed the rock on the ground and swung his other leg over so he was facing her she was at least reassured he wouldn't jump while she watched.

"I have no reason to live," he said.

"You're young, things might change and maybe the problem isn't quite as bad as you think? There must be people who care or would miss you."

He shook his head.

She prompted, "Family, friends, co-workers?"

"I've already proved too great a disappointment."

"I know it can feel as though no one cares, but it's not true. For one thing, I care." As Rebekah spoke, she realised she was repeating words her friends had said to her. Maybe there had been some truth in them?

"My name is Rebekah," she said and offered her hand.

After a moment's hesitation he shook it and said, "I am Etienne."

"Etienne, the man I loved no longer cares about me. I'd gone against my parents' wishes and the advice of my friends to be with him and it seemed that I had nothing left to live for. No lover, no home, no job, no future, no hope."

"You? But you are young and charming and forgive me, but you speak not only French?"

"I'm English."

"To speak another language is a talent, one which could provide a job. And your family and friends, they didn't want you to be with the man because they cared for your happiness. Perhaps they still do?"

"Yes, you are right. It's taken me a long time to see it, but I'm starting to understand that everything I said to you is true."

"For you."

"And maybe for you too?"

He shrugged again.

"You have a talent, Etienne?"

"Shall we have a coffee? There is somewhere nearby."

"All right, but perhaps you'd better move that rock. If someone walks over here in the dark…"

"You are right." He picked it up and dropped it down into the river. They both watched as it made a huge splash and sank down out of sight.

They walked quietly to a village so pretty and traditionally French it was hard to believe it wasn't a film set.

"Music, that is my talent," Etienne said once they were settled in the old fashioned cafe, sipping aromatic coffee. "I sing, play the guitar and write songs. My family say there is no future in that. They want me to be a doctor like my father. I will not make a good doctor, Rebekah." He told her that he was often invited to sing at parties and in bars. He could never refuse the opportunity of an audience and performed late into the night. As a result he was often tired and made mistakes in his training and knew he had little chance of qualifying. "Not that I want to, but my family do not believe that. It is hopeless."

"No it's not! You should follow your dreams."

"Like you with your dreams of love?"

"No, not that, but I hoped to be a teacher. I'm going to apply again to train for that." It wasn't until she said it she realised she'd made the decision.

"There will be love for you too, I think. You just have to wait and it will find you."

"I'll wait for love if you sing while I do."

He said nothing.

"Your family… would they rather their son was a trainee doctor drowned in the river, or a happy, even if struggling, musician."

"Perhaps you are right. Maybe I have not properly explained it to them."

They talked together all afternoon, drinking coffee and later sharing bread and cheese.

"I should go," Rebekah said. "I'm booked into a hotel and they'll be expecting me."

"I too have people who will expect me home. I have a great deal to tell them, I think. Will you meet me a year from now and see if either of us is closer to our dream?"

"Yes, yes I will."

Rebekah pulled cash from her pocket. "How much do I owe?"

He gave her euro notes a funny look. "I will pay." He

dropped a few coins onto a saucer.

A year later she'd returned to France in search of him and seen his photo on a record sleeve and listened to his song about their meeting. Of course it couldn't really be him. The singer must be her Etienne's grandfather, but in that case why would his family have been so against him becoming a musician?

Rebekah read the biographical information inside the cd case. 'Rebekah' was Etienne Dupont's first hit. He wrote the song based on a real meeting with a girl called Rebekah it said. There was another big hit, 'One Year On' about the same girl. With its release he'd become a commercial success. Two years later he'd married and later had children.

Rebekah listened to the second song. It spoke of his sadness that she'd not been on the bridge as they'd arranged and of his hope that one day he would see her again.

It didn't take her long to discover that the older Etienne still lived in the area and to learn of his address. She didn't quite know what she would say, or why she felt so compelled to meet him, but Rebekah found the address and knocked on the door.

An elderly lady answered.

"I was hoping to speak to Etienne?"

"My husband or my grandson?" the lady asked.

Rebekah wasn't sure what to say. "Whoever I met on the bridge."

"What is your name, child?"

"Rebekah."

The lady looked startled, but beckoned her inside.

Rebekah followed her down a hallway and into a sunlit room. An old man sat, seemingly asleep, in a wicker chair.

"Etienne, Rebekah is here."

He opened his eyes and smiled. The family resemblance to the young man she'd met was so strong she almost felt that she recognised him. He moved his hand slightly.

"Go, sit with him. I'll bring you coffee," his wife said.

When Rebekah hesitated she added, "Tell him your news. He's been waiting."

"Rebekah, it's really you?" the old man asked.

"I don't know. How can it be? I met Etienne Dupont a year ago, but your songs were written before I was born."

He gestured for her to come closer and studied her face. "It is you. I don't understand it myself, but there was something about that bridge… It's been the start of many good things for me."

"It didn't feel quite real when I was there, but being there, if I really was, and meeting you helped me too."

"So you have become a teacher?"

"Not yet, I'm still training. I'll get there though."

"And love?"

"You said if I waited then it would find me."

There was a tap on the door. "Grandfather?"

"Yes, come in, Etienne. There's someone here I think you should meet." He chuckled.

Rebekah looked round to see a man the same age as the Etienne she remembered. He looked almost identical, but she knew he wasn't the same man.

As she was being introduced, Mrs Dupont returned with coffee for them all. She explained how sixty years previously she'd seen Etienne sitting on a bridge as she'd walked to the village.

"He was still there when I returned hours later and said he was waiting for a girl he'd met the year before. I said it didn't look like she was coming, but he insisted she would and that love comes to those who wait."

"And I was right!" Etienne the musician said.

She nodded. "I said as he was waiting alone he was waiting for the wrong girl and eventually he agreed and married me."

The family insisted Rebekah stay with them and the younger Etienne helped her carry in her bags.

"I'm going to open a bottle of wine, come and join us when you're ready."

Rebekah spent three idyllic days as their guest, listening to the elder Etienne's music and the story of his life since he'd met an English girl on the old stone bridge. His wife cooked wonderful meals, sharing tips on the use of herbs to create traditional French recipes.

Rebekah breathed in the scent of marjoram and for a moment it seemed time had slipped again, but it was only in her memory she once again walked the path to the stone bridge. This time there was no sadness, no despair as she peeled and chopped vegetables. Their grandson spent all his free time showing her around the area and flirting with her over a glass or two of the delicious local wine.

He took her for a stroll along the river path and through what remained of the wood. It was an attractive, peaceful place if you ignored the muted rumble of traffic, very like where she'd walked a year before, but it wasn't exactly the same. For one thing, this time it felt real.

"I feel like I'm here under false pretences," she told him. "Obviously I'm not the person your grandfather met."

"He seems sure and he told us what he would have done that day if you hadn't stopped him, so we owe you a lot."

"You believe it then, that I somehow went back in time?"

He shrugged, just as she remembered the Etienne she'd met on the bridge doing.

"I don't," she said. "I'm sure there was a girl on the bridge, but it wasn't me. She said something which persuaded him to go on with his music and he wrote songs which are how he now remembers the incident. He said I'm exactly as he remembers, but would his recollection be so precise after all that time?"

He gave that familiar shrug again.

"And when he speaks about it, he mentions only what's in the song. Just that they both had dreams they wanted to pursue, that love would wait for them and that they'd meet again on the bridge. Yet they were together all afternoon. They must have spoken about other things, perhaps they shared a coffee or went for a walk… he doesn't remember, yet is positive my eyes are the exact shade as hers."

"Yes… but you remember it too, you came back to find him."

"I was very upset then and I think I somehow imagined it. I guess I'd once heard your grandfather's songs and daydreamed that I too would meet someone who'd persuade me to go in pursuit of what I wanted, and that somewhere love would find me if I waited for it."

By then they were close to the new bridge and the roar of the traffic meant that to be heard they had to walk so close their hands touched now and then. "And what you want is to teach? In England?"

"To teach, yes but whether it's teaching French to English

students, or helping French ones learn English, well, that's not so important."

He moved closer still and put his hand against her cheek. "And love? Has that found you?"

"I think perhaps it has."

In the shadow of the new bridge, Etienne kissed her.

7. Alarm Clock

Niall could hear the regular clicking of Georgia's old clock. Unfortunately it wasn't one of those antique pendulum kinds with a soothing tick tock. This one was digital, illuminated and annoying. It was hard to read at night, not like their new one which displayed the time by a powerful beam projected onto the ceiling.

The old alarm had numbers which clicked round every minute. That was just the wrong length interval. Perfect for a clock obviously, but not for a light sleeper in the same room. Just as Niall was almost nodding off there would be another click. Not quite enough to wake him, but just enough to stop him dropping off again when he awoke, like now in the small hours.

The clock had irritated Niall for a long time. At first he'd only spent the occasional night with Georgia, so it hadn't been a big problem. Certainly not enough to make him say something critical to the girl he was rapidly realising would be the love of his life. Then, when unable to get back to sleep, he'd filled the time thinking about their future.

When they were getting ready to move in together he should have just said he wasn't keen on the clock, but somehow the words didn't come out as intended and he asked how she'd come by it.

"Gran gave it to me."

That wasn't good news. She'd lost her gran not long before. In fact a small legacy from her had helped with the deposit on their home. Just then wasn't the time to complain about the clock. Maybe with hearing it every night he'd get used to it?

"It was when I first got my own place," Georgia continued. "Gran said I needed something like it."

"Wise woman, your gran," he remarked.

"Yes, took to you straight away, didn't she?"

"Actually I was referring to the fact that without an alarm you'd sleep to midday!" He remembered a couple of times when Georgia had stayed over with him on a weekend and done exactly that. Not that he'd minded as, once he'd made them some tea, he'd got back into bed with her.

"No doubt she had the practical aspects in mind, but she also said it would watch over me and keep me safe. When I wake up in the night and see the faint glow and hear the gentle click it's as though she's doing just that."

Of course Niall couldn't ask her to get rid of it after that. He did try to ignore it, or get used to it, or think of it as somehow watching over them, but it continued to irritate him. Actually it was worse once he knew he was stuck with it. He didn't wake up every night and the times he did he always got back to sleep eventually, so he put up with the old clock. Actually in the daytime he acknowledged that it probably only kept him awake for a few minutes, but in the dark it seemed as though he lay there awake for hours.

When he mentioned the clock, at a family gathering not long before their wedding, it hadn't been a premeditated attempt to get a replacement for it, but the hint was taken and they were given a new digital alarm. Georgia had seemed happy to use it and he'd been delighted both with her decision and the reason for it.

"I've got you to look out for me and keep me safe now," she'd said.

That was almost five years ago and through all that time the new, wedding gift clock gave reliable, silent service. It would still be doing that if Georgia hadn't got it into her head to swap it for the old one. He hadn't realised she had until he woke and heard that irritating click. He hadn't noticed it when he'd got into bed, but his attention was as usual on his gorgeous wife, what she had to say to him and things he wanted to tell her. It was their routine to discuss the day's events and bring to mind the positives before going to sleep.

Although not sure exactly when Georgia had made the change, he was fairly certain he knew why. She was heavily pregnant and not having an easy time of it. However Georgia lay she couldn't get comfortable, so slept only fitfully. Of course if the clock helped even the tiniest bit he was happy for her to have it by her side. It wasn't there though, he realised. He could still see the red numbers on the ceiling from the newer one and the click was quite faint. Perhaps she'd placed it in the nursery?

As Niall stepped out onto the top landing of their town house he heard an odd sound from downstairs. He went down both sets of stairs slowly, then raced back up when he realised what was wrong. There was a fire!

"Georgia, wake up," he said, gently shaking her with one hand and typing 999 on his phone with the other.

"What is it?" she mumbled.

Niall answered both her query and that of the emergency services operator at one. "There's a fire in our kitchen. My wife and I are leaving the house now." He gave their address as he grabbed warm clothes for Georgia and himself.

"Come on, love, hurry."

"You were lucky the kitchen door was shut," a fire officer told them the following day. "That kept the fire contained. It's a mess in there but the damage is mostly superficial. It's safe to go back in now."

Niall was relieved about the house, but he had even more reason to be glad he'd woken in the night and gone to investigate. The kitchen door was right by the bottom of the stairs. Left unchecked the fire would have burned through it. That would have set off the alarm in the hallway, but heat and smoke would have risen through the stairwell. They'd probably have had to jump from the bedroom window. Niall knew the fire brigade would have had something to catch them in, but the jump would have been terrifying for Georgia and potentially dangerous for the baby.

"How lucky I am," Georgia said.

"It could have been a lot worse," Niall agreed.

"Yes, but I wasn't just meaning the fire. I'm so lucky to have you watching over me and keeping me safe."

"Me and your gran."

"Gran? What does she have to do with it?"

"I must have woken just when the fire started, but I wouldn't have known about it if I didn't hear that old alarm clock she gave you."

"You can't have. It's in the attic and doesn't have batteries."

"It might not have been there, but I heard it. Maybe Gran was watching over you through me?"

"I'd like to believe that. It would mean she knew about the baby."

"Then believe it, love. Let's fetch the old clock down, shall we? I think it might help you sleep."

That night Georgia slept easily for the first time in weeks. That wasn't surprising after the drama of the fire.

Niall lay awake. That wasn't surprising either due to the lingering smell of smoke. He could hear the old clock clicking every minute. A gentle, soothing sound which sent him back to sleep feeling safe and protected.

8. Cecily's Doll

I hold the doll which I still think of as Cecily's, though it's twenty years since she gave it to me. Gently I move its limbs so it's down on one knee and holding out a hand. There's a length of gold thread on the table which I've fashioned into a tiny ring, but I don't reach for it.

The doll is dressed in jeans made from the spare material of those I took up for my boyfriend, Will. I created the rugby shirt from one Will accidentally ripped. I could have repaired it, but Will said it wasn't worth the effort.

That's what I do for a living; make and mend clothes. Usually for people, but I make some for Cecily's doll and toys belonging to my customers too. That's only right as it was the doll which got me started. Perhaps I should start at the beginning…

Cousin Cecily and I were playing tea parties in our gran's garden one sunny Easter. She, Cecily, lived a long way away but I saw her every school holiday. Even back then she wasn't really healthy, but was great fun to be around.

"I've got a magic doll," she told me.

"Let's see it then," I'd demanded. It looked ordinary to me. Dull even.

"With this, I can make people do whatever I want," Cecily said.

I believed that. People usually were willing to do

whatever she wanted. Certainly I was always happy to play any games she dreamed up.

"Go on then, show me," I coaxed.

She asked me for my hair ribbon which she wound around the doll, sari fashion. Cecily dabbed up a crumb of chocolate cake and fed it to the doll. Gran's chocolate cake was yummy, so I ate another slice.

Cecily grinned and wobbled the doll round in a kind of crazy dance. That looked fun so I copied the movements.

"See, told you!" Cecily laughed and I joined in.

"Can I try?"

When she handed it over I unwound the ribbon, then studied Cecily for something I could use.

"One of your socks should do." I scrambled over and slid it off her foot. There was a little ruff of lace at the top so, when I'd pulled it on the doll, it looked as though she were in a pretty sleeping bag. For a moment I stared at it, entranced by the difference a change of clothes could make, even when they were just pretend.

I moved the doll's arms around as though she was doing that signalling thing sailors do with flags.

Cecily copied every position. "It's working," she assured me.

The game didn't last long. She was soon tired and her dad came and carried her in.

The following summer Cecily and I watched gymnastics on TV. I had one of those sweatbands on my wrist, just like my favourite gymnast. Cecily put that on the doll's hair, securing it into a ponytail. Then she had me doing forward roll, handstands, star jumps and the bridge. Neither the doll nor I were much good at any of them, except the bit where you stand still at the end. By then Cecily couldn't even manage that.

Once I told her about a school bully. "She calls me awful names and scribbled in my books," I said. "I can't prove it was her, but I know it was."

"Have you got any here?" Cecily asked.

I had because my parents insisted I do homework even at Gran's.

"Do you need this page?" Cecily asked.

"I suppose not."

Carefully, Cecily ripped it into a rough circle, then folded it into a point. Her hands weren't strong enough to tear through the folded paper, so I did that bit. Cecily put the paper poncho onto the doll and made it walk away, along the arm of her chair. The bully never bothered me again.

As we grew up, we played with the doll less, but Cecily always had it with her, tucked into the side of her chair. When I was worried about my exams, Cecily wrote B A* A on a piece of notepaper, put it into the doll's hand and said, "Well done, Anne! Great grades."

I got mostly Cs but also managed a B, A and A*. As she'd been helping with my revision, Cecily probably guessed how well I'd do.

"Can't we use the doll to make you well?" I asked her again.

"No. It can make people do things, but it can't change who they are," she told me.

I didn't know then why she was so sure it wouldn't help her, but looking back I guess maybe she'd tried… Just as I did the few times I got hold of the doll without her seeing. Once I got it to lift weights, hoping that would make her stronger. Cecily slept for the rest of that day. I gave it pretend medicine. That was no more effective than the real stuff she'd dutifully swallowed so much of. I powdered its cheeks with blusher to give it a healthy glow. Cecily looked beautiful, yet remained as fragile as ever.

She was in hospital a lot after I left school. When I visited she was often wearing a surgical gown. That wasn't in readiness for operations; they couldn't have cured her. Cecily needed help with almost everything and the gowns made it easier for her carers.

As I had plenty of free time on my hands, I made Cecily some new clothes, using a gown for a pattern. Simple long tunics with velcro fastening, so they were easy to take on and off. Instead of boring white, I chose bright patterns I knew she'd love. The offcuts I used to make dresses for the doll, which she still took with her everywhere.

That's how my dressmaking business really took off. I'll make clothes for anyone, but specialise in those for people with different needs. I can make them with fastenings anywhere and of any type, accommodate non-standard body shapes, prosthetics or appliances, use easily washable fabrics – anything which makes life a little easier for the wearer or whoever helps them. I love that I'm always asked for pretty designs and bright, uplifting colours. But I'm getting ahead of myself…

Cecily's condition worsened as we all knew it would. She was often in pain, something she'd largely been spared until then.

"I want you to take my doll," she told me. She said it as though it was important, despite having told me several times over the years that I was to have it after she died.

I tried to reassure her. "Don't worry, everyone knows that

and I'll take good care of it."

"Now, Anne. Take it now. Please."

"No. Not yet."

"Please. It hurts so much…"

I took the doll home, laid it gently on a pillow and smoothed its hair. "Sleep now," I whispered.

Cecily slipped away that night.

She must have known she didn't have long and wanted to give me the doll herself.

For a long time the doll sat on my dressing table wearing the dress I'd made to match one of Cecily's hospital gowns. Sometimes I'd talk to it, as though it were Cecily, and imagine what she'd say in reply to push away my minor annoyances or worries. Often that was enough to make me smile.

I was working in a sweatshop then. Well, factory really, but that's what we all called it. We made clothes, as quickly and cheaply as possible. We were all on minimum wage and treated as though we weren't worth even that. One day someone saw a report of the company's annual profits and said we should get a share.

"We should write to the papers," one colleague suggested. Another thought we should form a union. Someone else suggested we kidnap the boss and hold him to ransom. We ruled that out, but decided we'd all try something, even if it was no more than asking nicely. That, it was decided, was to be my job.

The boss listened, or pretended to. He droned on about overheads, capital, rent, and said he was only just making ends meet himself.

Later I saw his jacket draped carelessly over a chair. He

was only just making ends meet in top-of-the-range designer clothes. Without thinking, I whisked the handkerchief from his top pocket. Real silk, with his initials on. I heard someone coming, and fearing I'd be caught, quickly stuffed it in my bag.

That evening I remembered the games Cecily and I had played – and that I still had the handkerchief. I draped it around the doll, like an oversized cape, then put a five pence coin in each of the doll's hand. Imitating the boss's voice as well as I could, I announced all staff were to have a pay rise.

A week later, the man himself did the same thing; and made so much fuss you'd think he was a cape wearing superhero. One and a half percent we got. Weirdly, when the new rates were calculated, my monthly salary was no longer an amount in whole pounds, but included an odd ten pence too.

I kept thinking about what the boss had said. It was true he had the expenses he'd listed, but he still made a profit. If I set up my own business in my parent's spare room, I wouldn't have many overheads to worry about. So that's exactly what I did.

Cecily's doll was relocated into my new workroom and seemed to encourage me. Having it there made me think of contacting hospitals and health charities, with the idea of making practical yet attractive clothing for people who found it difficult to dress themselves. I also did alterations and repairs. I loved the variety. One day I'd be hemming curtains for a neighbour, the next making prosthesis friendly sun dresses or repairing brocade drapes for the swanky hotel in town. I had several regular customers, including Will. He had a talent for buying clothes which didn't quite fit. Nearly every week I was taking up a pair of trousers, letting out or taking in seams or adjusting sleeves.

"It's not just coincidence is it?" I asked Cecily's doll. It was wearing a pretty dress at the time. I couldn't remember when I'd last changed its outfit. In fact I'd paid it very little attention for ages. Just for fun, or so I told myself, I made it a new outfit with cut offs from things I'd altered for Will.

Grinning to myself I cut out a tiny pink rose from a scrap of patterned material and slipped it into the doll's hand. I made it walk towards me, then in a deep voice said, "Anne, will you go out with me?"

When Will asked me out he brought daisies not roses, but they were pink.

We've been going out together now for nearly two years. I love Will and want to spend the rest of my life with him. I made the doll a tiny wedding dress from lace left over from a blouse I stitched for myself and which Will especially likes. I'm sure it will fit, but I haven't tried it on the doll. It's still wearing the jeans and shirt made from pieces of Will's clothes. It's down on one knee, just as I posed it, and there's a tiny circle of gold thread within reach. I could easily put it in the doll's hand and act out a proposal. I don't though. It's not that I think doing that would really make anything happen or that I believe it really is magic. It's my dear cousin Cecily's doll and important only for the memories associated with it.

Besides, Will is taking me to my favourite restaurant tonight and he's said there's something important he wants to ask me.

9. Awfully Nice Neighbours

When it became clear that whoever was knocking wasn't going to give up easily, Laura was the one to give in. She went to the door and looked through the peephole. It was her neighbour. She'd know Laura was in, so not answering wasn't an option and Laura opened the door.

"Would you like to see our puppy?" Mrs Anderson asked.

"Um. I…" For a minute an image of Sporran, the Scottie dog she'd been given when she was a schoolgirl flashed into Laura's mind. How she'd loved him.

"Please do come," Mrs Anderson urged. "I'm sure you'll like him. And you can have a cup of tea. Dave's just bought some currant buns from the bakery."

Laura didn't want to be sociable, but how could she refuse without seeming rude or ungrateful? They'd been very kind since Giles had died. Checking she was OK, offering lifts and meals. If she stroked the dog and ate a bun they might think they'd done their duty and leave her in peace for a few days.

"I'll come round in a few minutes."

Laura stared at her reflection in the hallway mirror. At least her clothes were clean, even if they were Giles's. There wasn't much she could do for her hair, but a dab of lipstick and dusting of powder made her look a bit less sickly.

The puppy was nothing like Sporran. He'd been neat,

black and calm. This one, though tiny, had gangly limbs and trembled with excitement. His great plume of a tail wagged so fast it was nothing but a blur.

"We got him from a rescue centre," Julie Anderson explained. "Someone's dog got pregnant without them realising and they couldn't cope with all the pups. We've called him Caramac."

It was a good name. Laura stroked the soft, gingery fur and fondled his floppy ears. "He seems happy to be here."

"We hope he will be. We're taking a few days off work while he settles in and he'll have the run of the garden while we're at work. We've put in a cat flap and he's already getting the hang of it."

"It will be nice having a dog next door," Laura said. He seemed a sweet little thing, even if it was impossible to guess what breed either of its parents had been.

"If you want to borrow him for walks or anything…"

"Oh no. I couldn't." Laura didn't leave the house except for her weekly shopping trip. That left her breathless and shaking.

When she got back home, Laura put a load of clothes in the washing machine and then washed her hair. Next time Julie Anderson knocked on the door she wouldn't look quite such a fright and maybe the neighbours would stop feeling obliged to keep an eye on her. It was kind, but she preferred to be left alone.

Rather than them offering her help, there was something she could do for them. Laura sorted out clothes and newspapers to give her neighbours. They'd said anything like that would be useful while they were housetraining Caramac. All Giles's gardening clothes and magazines were gradually transferred next door. It took days. Although the Andersons insisted she drink a cup of tea on each trip, Laura felt better for having a clear out.

Throwing out her husband's things had seemed wrong, but somehow giving them away like that didn't. Maybe it was due to the ecstasies Caramac went into whenever he saw her. He seemed to love attention.

When the Andersons went back to work, Caramac started yapping all day every day. It wasn't loud, but it was heartbreaking. It reminded her of Sporran. It was uncanny how alike they sounded considering they weren't even the same breed and weren't similar in any other way. Her little Scottie had made life bearable after her mother died and been her companion for nearly twenty years, right up until his death just before her marriage to Giles. Caramac wasn't Sporran and with his barking he was making her life worse, not better.

If she went out into her garden and spoke to him he was quiet; all she could hear was the sound of his feet as he ran around and around in tiny circles. He looked so funny she couldn't help laughing. She didn't want to stand out there all day though and as soon as she went back indoors he started up his pitiful yapping again.

Laura tried telling the Andersons, but she doubted they believed her. Caramac hardly made a sound when they were there. When they left for work, he yapped incessantly. Most people in the street worked during the day so, as far as she knew, Laura was the only person to hear him. Caramac gave an excited bark when his owners came home, or when Laura went out in her garden to hang washing, but that was quite different.

When she next forced herself to go shopping, Laura

bought a big bag of dog chews. It meant spending longer out the house than usual, but she managed it. As she called Caramac and threw him a chew he gave a little bark. She frowned; sometimes he didn't sound like her old dog at all. Of course he wasn't her Sporran and really she shouldn't feed him without asking. She did that as soon as the Andersons came home.

"Oh yes, that's fine and very kind of you," Julie Anderson said.

"No chocolate though," Dave added.

Laura promised it would just be proper dog chews and just one a day. She stuck to that but they didn't keep Caramac quiet for long. It was getting harder to listen to him. The noise didn't disturb her in the way it would if, say, someone were constantly hammering or using loud machinery. In a way it was worse. It was as though Sporran were stuck somewhere, desperately trying to get to her. She should go out and look for him.

Laura threw on another sweater and her coat. Pausing by the back door she took a big breath, then rushed out before the familiar panic could make her legs give way. The sooner she found him the sooner she'd be home warm and safe. She'd been striding out for twenty minutes before she stopped in her tracks. It was Caramac she'd heard yapping of course, not Sporran. The dog wasn't trapped or hurt, just a bit noisy. What had she been thinking? Laura turned and walked home. It wasn't until she was inside, sipping tea she realised she wasn't shaking from the shock of leaving the house as she usually was those days. She didn't hear Caramac again that day until he barked once to welcome his owners home.

The following day, after lunch, Laura decided to try going

for another short walk. The doctor had said it would do her good to get out more and she'd slept better the previous night than she had in some time. The moment she made the decision, Caramac stopped yapping.

Over the next few weeks, Laura took gradually longer walks. She looked at the snowdrops, then early daffodils in people's gardens as she passed. People sometimes greeted her, or exchanged a few words about the weather. She lost her terror of leaving home. She felt almost human once more.

That was right up until the anniversary of Giles's death. His loss hit her again. Never again would she write him a birthday card, or one for Christmas or their anniversary. Never again would she get one from him. Laura wanted to go back to sleep and forget. She couldn't though; Caramac was yapping away even more frantically than usual. She had to get away from that.

It was sleeting, but Laura didn't bother with a coat or hat. Being cold and wet wouldn't make her any more miserable. She wasn't sure if the moisture on her face was teardrops or slushy snow as she pulled the back door shut and turned to throw Caramac a chew so she wouldn't have to hear that pitiful sound as she walked away.

As she swung her arm, Laura's foot slid from under her and she fell. She heard a crack and the breath was knocked from her as she crashed down. Caramac's yapping continued at a frantic level. There was something wrong about that… it was Saturday. The Andersons would be home and anyway, the dog stayed inside when it rained. Why then, when Laura just wanted to close her eyes and drift away, did he have to yap?

Then she heard a single bark. Caramac must have spotted

his chew and dashed out to grab it, and was barking to say thank you. Funny how she could tell, or thought she could tell, what all those similar sounding barks meant. It had been the same with Sporran. Laura had always felt she understood the gist of what he was saying. All except that one time when Laura's appendix had burst. She'd woken in too much pain to even call for help but Sporran had woken Dad with his yapping. A sound just like Caramac was making now. Except he wasn't, he was still giving his 'hello, Laura thanks for the chew' bark. That was escalating into a 'why aren't you answering?' and then up into a worried howl. The yapping was still going on too.

Laura knew then why it had disturbed her so much and why no one else had heard it. Caramac hadn't been the one yapping, it was Sporran. He knew she was in trouble after Giles' death and was calling for help. She'd never been able to reach him or stop him because it had been her in need of that help. Now she needed it more than ever and two dogs were calling for it.

Laura felt something soft and wet on her cheek. Sporran, had he found her at last? No, it was Caramac.

"Laura! Hold on Laura, we've called an ambulance," Dave Anderson said.

Julie placed a thick coat over her. "Don't try to move, they'll be here soon."

Laura was warm and dry when she awoke. All around was a mechanical buzzing, but the absence of a yapping dog made it seem eerily quiet. She struggled to sit up. Hospital. She had fallen and was in hospital.

"There's nothing seriously wrong," she was told. "You were in shock so we kept you overnight, but I expect once the doctor's had a look at you you can go home."

That proved to be the case. Julie Anderson phoned to see how she was and came to collect her.

"You gave us a fright," Julie said.

"Gave myself one too. Thought I'd broken my hip or something."

"No, just your key fob. We found them under you when they lifted you on to a stretcher."

Julie used those same keys to open Laura's front door, before helping her out the car and inside. "Is there anything you need, anything I can do?"

"There's just one thing. Can I borrow Caramac while you're at work? I'd like the company and once the bruising has gone, I could take him for walks."

"He'd love that, I'm sure."

Laura only heard Sporran once more. He gave a single happy sounding yap as though to say he approved.

10. Afternoon Tea

Lydia pours fragrant tea into the delicate cup. The last unchipped one from the set which her parents had as a wedding present. She adds sugar from the bowl which matches, and pours milk from the jug which doesn't quite. It's all blue and white though; the crockery and her age twisted hands.

Two chocolate biscuits, the good kind, are balanced on the saucer. Carefully she carries her treat into the living room. Her favourite symphony plays on the stereo. She sits and a quiet contented sigh escapes her lips. It's the last breath she'll ever exhale.

The tea cools untasted.

11. Gone By Boxing Day

"A small reward for you," Lin said as she handed Harold a glass of sherry.

"I thought we were saving this for Christmas? Not that I'm complaining."

"It feels as though Christmas is coming early. We're doing really well with the presents this year. The ones I've bought are already wrapped and I've just had an email to say everything I've bought on the internet has been despatched, so I'm feeling quite festive."

"Great!" said Harold who hated to see his wife stressed out over the Christmas shopping. He hated her to worry almost as much as he hated getting involved with the shopping himself. He detested battling through packed, overheated shops that blasted Christmas songs at him. He became irritated at being constantly accosted by excessively jolly people in red who waved charity collecting tins at him.

He didn't mind giving some change; there were plenty of people, animals too, in need of food or shelter and he wanted to help them. The problem was that he always had his hands full and had to pull off his gloves and search through his pockets and he always dropped things and then his shopping got mixed up. He wouldn't remember whether he'd got everything and he'd go back for a few things just in case. Then he'd spot the perfect present for someone whom he'd just bought a gift for. That had been the first thing he'd seen that was remotely suitable. So, he bought the perfect thing, but then realised that meant he'd spent more on one child than the others so bought more to even things up. Then he'd come out and the tin rattlers had changed shifts and in the crush at the tills he'd lost the stickers showing he'd given, so he'd had to juggle even more bags as he searched for change and hoped the car park ticket hadn't expired yet.

There was no need to get worked up, he remembered. Luckily this year, Lin had got everything done while he worked overtime to pay for it and he was spared the dreaded visit to the shopping centre. Harold took another sip of his sherry and sighed with satisfaction.

Lin said, "I am pleased with how organised I've been. I've even made a cake and put a couple of batches of mince pies into the freezer."

"Marvellous!" said Harold who was very partial to home-made Christmas cake and mince pies.

"There's just one gift left to buy," Lin said in a carefully casual tone. "Maybe you could get it while I put up the decorations, make brandy butter and take the neighbours' cards round?" She gave a him hopeful smile.

It sounded such a reasonable request. It probably was a reasonable request, yet still it filled him with dread. He gulped. "Er, is this final gift for my mother?"

"Yes it is, actually." Lin's tone was now slightly more careful and a bit less casual, but she kept her hopeful smile in place.

He was sure he knew the answer to his next question, but he asked it anyway. "Have you thought of something suitable?"

If she, or anyone else, had then it would be a first. His daughter had asked for suggestions just a few days ago.

"Gran's already got anything that would be suitable," Julie complained. "Every time I have an idea, I visit Gran and see her wearing or using whatever I've thought of."

Harold had agreed. "Mum buys whatever she wants herself. I wish she'd just tell us what she'd like, but she says it's no fun unless it's a surprise."

Finding a suitable gift for Harold's mum was a problem for the whole family. Harold's dad often joked, during one of the regular family discussions on the subject, that he just went into the first clothes shop he found and asked for anything they had for the price he wanted to pay.

"They ask what type of garment and I say it doesn't matter. They ask what size and colour, I say that doesn't matter I just need something to wrap and a receipt so she can bring it back and change it. You definitely need to keep the receipt whatever it is, money up in smoke otherwise."

Harold's brother confessed he usually bought her present in a charity shop.

"Why not? It'll end up there anyway," he said.

"Or she'll give it to someone else to look after it for her," Lin had remarked.

Lin had sometimes picked gifts her sister-in-law would like as she knew her birthday was in January and Harold's mother often recycled unwanted Christmas gifts by wrapping them in birthday paper and giving them as an extra present to her daughter.

Remembering these remarks was no help to Harold. He considered buying gift vouchers, but he couldn't do it. His mum always loved to receive beautifully wrapped gifts and to open them after Christmas lunch. She said it was so exciting to see what was inside and she appreciated the trouble people had gone to even if she never, ever, kept what she was given. She was always generous and thoughtful when she bought gifts too. He had to buy her something.

He thought of really carrying through his dad's idea of getting anything at all plus a receipt, but all the clothing shops were so busy he couldn't face going in for something he knew wasn't right. The charity shop wasn't so busy, maybe he could get something to unwrap and give her vouchers too? That might have been acceptable, but there was nothing remotely suitable for Mum. He did find a vase in the exact colour of the curtains his daughter had just made for her new flat so he bought that for her. He also bought a book he thought his dad would like and told the cashier there was no need for change.

"That's very generous of you, sir," she said, taking the note that Harold only then realised was larger than the one he'd meant to offer. Oh well, that'd see someone hungry got a good meal or two, he didn't begrudge it.

When he walked down the street and saw someone with a tin for the same charity, Harold decided he'd done enough. Instead of wrestling with gloves and bags he crossed the street to avoid the girl. At least he tried to. Instead he tripped over the curb and fell down, banging his head. He saw stars for a few seconds and all the thoughts about Mum's present seemed to be circling around in his head before people rushed to see if he was hurt. After a moment to think about it he realised he wasn't. Better yet, the red glass vase was unbroken and better still he'd had a very bright idea about Mum's present.

Concerned people were eager to call an ambulance to get him checked over or give him hot sweet tea for shock or make him go into shops and lie down or to give him a lift home. Harold hadn't realised there were so many things that could be done for someone who'd fallen over, nor that there were so many kind people willing to do them. He didn't want a fuss made though, it was worse than getting through the tills while harassed assistants asked if he wanted batteries and insurance and gift wrap.

"I'm going to my daughter's flat just over there," he said escaping all but one of the good Samaritans. That young man insisted on walking with him.

"I don't want to inconvenience you," Harold said. "You must have Christmas shopping to do?"

"No problem. My family are going away for Christmas so I gave them their presents of foreign currency for spending money last week and haven't any shopping left to do."

Harold guessed his daughter wouldn't mind if he arrived bearing a gift and a kind, attractive young man. On the way, after admitting the flat wasn't quite as close as he'd implied, he told the man about his idea for Mum's gift; he thought it was best to check with someone who hadn't just banged their head.

"That's brilliant!" the man said.

The man, Martin, drank a cup of tea with Harold and his daughter. Harold's hands didn't shake, his vision wasn't blurred, nothing hurt and he hadn't been knocked out so Jill and Martin decided he was fit to continue with the shopping. Martin left Jill his phone number and Harold left the vase.

Harold bought his mum's gift and went home.

"Any luck?" Lin asked.

"Yes. What do you think of this?" He showed her the contents of his very large carrier bag.

"Oh, Harold! That's a funny thing to give anyone for Christmas."

"Oh." Harold had been so sure it was a good idea.

"I don't know though, I think your mum will like it. Yes, I'm sure she will. I was thinking, while you were out, that the gifts she buys us might be a clue to what she'd like herself. She often gets things that are bright and shiny."

"That's true and at least we've got something to wrap and I've kept the receipt. When I explained what it was for, the man promised our money back if she didn't want it."

"That's OK, then." Lin laughed. "And at least she won't be saying she's already got one!"

On Christmas Eve, Jill rang to ask if she could bring a guest for lunch. "That nice young man Martin who helped you when you fell."

"Of course, I'd be delighted to see him again," Harold said after checking with Lin that there was enough food.

"You never told me what you got for Gran, and Martin won't say. Is it a surprise?"

"Yes, I think your gran will be surprised." He smiled to himself. Mum would be happy to be surprised and she'd love the pretty wrapping paper and gorgeous red velvet bow Lin had used. It wouldn't matter really if she thought the present was odd and asked to exchange it.

Harold's brother was the first to arrive at the house on Christmas day. "Keep the receipt for Mum's present did you?" he asked.

Harold said that he had.

"Good man. No one wants to see their money going up in smoke!"

Harold laughed, only a little nervously.

"Heard there's yet another charity shop in town, I hope whatever you've bought your mother doesn't end up there," Harold's brother-in-law said when he arrived.

"That's not very likely," Harold said. Impossible in fact, the seller would be the only person who could take Mum's gift off his hands if she didn't like it.

"Come on, I bet you she's got rid of whatever it is by Boxing Day."

Harold didn't risk taking the bet.

Mum was polite about all her gifts but there was, as usual, a general feeling that no one had yet got it quite right. She said the gloves from Jill were nice, but didn't take them out of the cellophane. She praised the boots her husband had bought, but didn't remove the tag that held them together so she could try them on. She said the whisky Harold's brother had bought would keep her warm, but didn't take off the top and take a sniff.

Harold handed over his gift.

"Good gracious, what a big box and so beautifully wrapped! Thank you, Harold and you too, Lin." Mum carefully removed the paper and bow Lin had used to make it look pretty.

"Well that's certainly a surprise!" Mum said.

Harold winked at Lin. Everyone leant forward, vainly trying to see what was in the package.

"I've never had anything like this before," Mum said.

Harold grinned at Lin.

There was a pause. Harold knew what everyone expected would come next. "I'll save it for later" or "it's too nice to use" or gently putting it to one side and a glance to see if there might still be a gift in someone's hand or under the tree that would actually be what she wanted. Mum did put the gift to one side, and she did look round but no one was holding out a gift and there was nothing under the tree.

"Oh, I almost forgot," Martin said and took a small gift from his pocket. "This is for you."

"That's very kind, young man. Especially as you don't even know me."

"Your son and granddaughter have spoken of you in such a way that I feel as though I do."

Mum removed the ribbon, remarking what a lovely colour it was. She opened the package to reveal an ordinary box of matches.

"Oh how clever! That's exactly what I wanted. The perfect gift! Thank you so much."

Some of the assembled crowd looked as though they thought she was overdoing it. Some looked puzzled, some pointed out she didn't smoke or have a gas cooker.

"Exactly and neither do Harold or Lin which is why I so needed the matches."

Harold's smile had turned to a beaming grin.

"Harold and Lin," Mum said, "Would you mind very much if your lovely gift was gone by Boxing Day? I'd so like us to use it now and share it with everyone."

Harold tried to say that was fine, but he was interrupted by his brother and Jill both demanding to know what it was.

"Surely you all know? No? Well, you'll get a bright shiny surprise too then, when Harold's money goes up in smoke.

Jill, pass me those lovely gloves you gave me dear; I think I'll need them." She turned to Harold's brother, "The whisky you bought, put it in the beautiful hip flask your dad gave me last year and that I gave Harold to, er, look after for me. And the boots you gave me this year," she told her husband, "now would be an excellent time to try them."

Although bemused, her family scurried around complying with her requests. Harold smiled at the sparkle in their eyes. Partly it was anticipation of Mum's shiny surprise, but he guessed they'd also be happy to realise their own gifts for Mum hadn't been wrong at all, it had just needed the right circumstances for them to be useful.

Once fully equipped with all her other gifts, Harold's mum and the rest of the family went out into the garden to watch the dazzling display from Harold and Lin's gift of fireworks.

12. Ethan's Investigations

Ethan squeezed Katya's hand as they waited in the darkness. He'd had reports of a variety of weird things happening in one quiet seaside town. The most promising had been the allegation that ghost children haunted the school in the summer holidays. Ethan had set out to investigate at his first opportunity.

As so often, his wife accompanied him. As always, he was grateful of her support. They made a great team. Often the leads sent to Ethan were hoaxes or dead ends, but the pointless waiting became a pleasure rather than a chore with Katya by his side. When there was something to see Katya photographed it for him. Her abilities with a camera were little short of miraculous. Even in the worst of conditions she never failed to capture an image to illustrate his reports.

"Did you see that?" Ethan pointed to what he thought was movement in the gloom.

"Where? Oh, yes. Yes. I'm sure there's something there." Katya raised her camera.

Just as the old lady who'd written to him had said, ghostly shapes began to appear in the school playing field.

Katya took several shots. "In this light the best you're likely to get is a spooky blur, unless whatever it is comes really close," she warned him.

That wasn't a problem. Ghostly blurs were quite popular

with some of the papers he sold his stories to. It seemed many people shared Ethan's interest in the unexplained.

This time though, there was no mystery to share. As the pale shapes seemed to float towards them, Ethan realised what they were. He laughed.

"What's so funny?" Katya asked.

"The idea of my informant watching them arrive one by one and that keeping her awake. They're sheep!"

"Oh! So they are."

The animals were very tame and allowed Katya to get close enough to use her flash. "They've got ear tags in, so we should be able to trace the owner."

It didn't take Ethan long to discover that the enterprising school caretaker let out the neighbouring farmer's sheep at night during the holidays to save him mowing the grass.

"I do a part time job at the golf course and keep the school's ride-on mower there over August," he admitted.

Long hours of sunlight and the popularity of the area as a tourist spot meant the golf course was always busy throughout the day in August, so he cut the grass at night. That explained the strange lights which had been seen by some people after an extra late night at a local club. It also made sense of the farmer's reports that his sheep sometimes temporarily vanished.

"I reported it to the police, but as the sheep had always reappeared unharmed by the time an officer came to investigate, they never took me seriously," the farmer had emailed Ethan.

He wouldn't have taken much interest himself had it not been for the other reports in the same area. Now he could at least reassure the farmer he wasn't imagining things.

As the mystery was solved more quickly than expected, Ethan and Katya stayed on in the hotel for a short holiday. They couldn't go paddling in the sea of course, because of his allergy, but they did other touristy things such as eating ice cream and fish and chips, listening to a band play in the winter garden, and looking around the castle.

"Sorry it didn't work out, love," he told Katya.

"It doesn't matter. Actually it's probably better. I'm getting a nice holiday instead of watching you work."

Bless her, she was always so loyal. She stayed by his side even when he was typing on his computer all day. This time there wasn't a story to sell. The caretaker was a widower working hard to support his children and Ethan and Katya didn't want to get him into trouble. The times the farmer thought his sheep vanished coincided with the overworked caretaker falling asleep and being late letting them back into their field and meant they were missed by the early rising farmer.

"Now I know what's happening, I don't mind," he said. "Grazing is always short in August, so I'm happy for the sheep to get a little extra."

Ethan wasn't too disappointed with the simple explanation of this and most of his other missions. The trips were always interesting. Often he did get some kind of story even if he never came close to finding proof of UFOs, ghosts or anything else not of this world. Katya too always seemed happy whatever the outcome and helped him search out possible leads.

Not all their investigations were as pleasant as the seaside sheep. Soon afterwards they had numerous reports of lights regularly seen in the sky over one particular area. Informants differed on whether these were caused by alien spaceships or ghostly visitations but everyone agreed they couldn't be planes, laser lights, kids pulling a prank or any of the other rational suggestions Ethan put forward.

"They're totally silent and all move together as though instructed or controlled by something powerful," one woman said.

"And if it's all so innocent, what about the fires and deaths?" one man demanded.

That got Ethan's attention. He discovered there had indeed been an alarming numbers of heath and farm fires as well as animal deaths. Cattle, wild deer and even exotic creatures in the safari park had become victims. A comparative search in different areas showed that these all occurred far more frequently than would normally be expected.

"Coincidence?" Katya tentatively suggested. She was good at playing devil's advocate and helped him weed out the stories which weren't worth looking into.

"I don't think so. As well as being more frequent than usual, all the deaths and fires occur very soon after the strange lights are seen. Often the person reporting one thing knew nothing about the other."

"Is someone doing it deliberately?"

"I doubt it." In his years as a journalist he had come across far too many unpleasant people doing horrible things, but that didn't seem to be the case this time. It didn't seem likely that a human had broken into the lion enclosure, or tangled with a rhino, but the vet reported none of the deaths were natural.

"We'd best get down there then. I'll book us a hotel," Katya said.

There weren't many options as although the area where

sightings had been reported was quite large, it was also mainly rural with no towns nearby. Her choice of accommodation was fortunate. On their first night a wedding reception was held and guests released candle lanterns just as it grew dark. They looked so pretty and romantic, drifting off together in the light breeze. Katya took a beautiful photograph of the lights hovering above the happy couple.

A quick check the next morning confirmed that every sighting of the mysterious lights coincided with a wedding reception and that the hotel routinely provided lanterns as part of the celebrations.

Usually the lights went straight up and weren't seen by anyone other than the people who released them and therefore knew what they were. Occasionally though, the wind caught them and took them over farms, houses or the safari park. Sometimes they landed or were blown onto buildings whilst still alight resulting in fires. The metal frames inside them were occasionally eaten by grazing animals causing a nasty death.

When Ethan and Katya proved the connection they were no longer welcome to stay on in the hotel which was facing bad publicity and possible prosecution. Ethan sold his story then and started up a campaign to try to ban the lanterns. A few people who cared about wildlife supported him, but he got an angry response from those who either profited from the lanterns or had used them in marking a happy event or to say goodbye to a loved one. He didn't mind that it made him unpopular as long as he still had Katya's support.

Ethan, despite talking to people professionally, was a bit of a loner. At school his severe allergy meant he was shunned by other kids. He understood now that they were a bit scared of him. So much was it impressed upon them they mustn't get him wet for fear of the terrible consequences that no one wanted to be near him. They wouldn't sit with him at lunchtimes or invite him to their parties in case they knocked over a drink. Of course he didn't go on swimming trips or use the poster paints mixed with water and never even went to school on days when it rained.

His parents were over protective he supposed, probably because he'd been an only child who'd come to them very late in life. They tried to make up for his missed education and lack of friends by providing him with plenty to read, and of course it was them who'd had to deal with the consequences when he did get wet.

Perhaps it was all the stories he read, or maybe his own feeling of being different which led to Ethan's obsession in ghosts and aliens. After a school lesson which taught his class of the importance of water for life and that a person's body is around three-quarters water, Ethan got teased worse than before. He could understand why they believed he, who couldn't touch the stuff, couldn't really be human.

Starting work didn't ease Ethan's isolation. Colleagues were very scornful of his journalistic abilities. He missed what seemed, to them, interesting storylines to follow up possible UFO leads.

"How can you fall for all that rubbish?" one asked.

"I don't fall for it. I investigate to see if the claims are true."

"Half an ounce of common sense should make that clear."

Sometimes that was indeed the case. Ethan quickly dismissed a report of a strange track through a cornfield when he realised it was in a straight line from the housing estate to the nearest shops and that people were just taking a short cut. No story there, but Ethan did make something of the claim Elvis was working in a chip shop. Unsurprisingly the man was in fact an Elvis impersonator doing a part time job. He was rather good and owed an improvement in his prospects to Ethan getting him not just into the papers, but singing on the radio. As a thank you he'd sung at Ethan and Katya's wedding reception.

The fact that Ethan exposed hoaxes and sold stories did nothing to win round other journalists. Ethan was given the nickname Extra Terrestrial Hunter And Nutter. He'd told Katya.

She said, 'Not nutter, newshound. People often mock what they don't understand."

That was true. His parents had said much the same thing after he was teased at school. He'd confided to one boy, whom he'd considered a friend, what happened if he got wet. He'd explained that meant he could only rarely have a normal wash and instead cleaned himself with special wipes and lotions. The boy had told everyone, exaggerating along the way. Ethan was called stinky, swampy and all kinds of horrible names. He'd been so hurt by the name calling and the betrayal that his parents had moved home so he could go to a different school. He learned his lesson and never told anyone more than was absolutely necessary, keeping the allergy a secret when he could.

Katya, of course, knew the truth. He wasn't quite sure how she'd come into his life. She just seemed to arrive. He'd come home one day after another unsuccessful attempt to find a job somewhere he could be sure of never getting wet. One he could do from home whenever there was the slightest chance of rain, and she was there drinking tea with his parents.

For Ethan it had been love at first sight. She'd been so easy to talk to and hadn't seemed phased about his allergy.

'It's aquagenic urticaria, isn't it?' she asked. That she used the proper medical name showed she took it seriously.

"I was reading about it in the newspaper," she told him. "There was a report about a young woman who developed it during pregnancy. Poor lady couldn't wipe away her little boy's tears for fear of them touching her skin and blistering it into a painful rash. Obviously your case is different."

"Yes, I've always had it. I think that's right, Mum?"

She confirmed that it was. "Of course we didn't know what triggered it then. We nearly lost you in those first weeks."

Ethan knew the story of course, but as he listened to it, repeated for Katya, he once again marvelled at what his parents had gone through and how lucky he was to be their son. Ethan's parents had taken a holiday shortly before he arrived. They'd gone off for some peace and quiet in their campervan.

"You can imagine our shock when you arrived during a thunderstorm!" Mum said.

"That doesn't sound at all peaceful," Katya said.

"It wasn't," Dad confirmed.

Ethan had almost forgotten that part. It was a good thing the children at school hadn't known, or they would have added Frankenstein to the list of names they called him.

When he realised he wanted to marry Katya, Ethan knew he'd have to share the full extent of his allergies with her. Remembering the reaction of his school friend he couldn't bring himself to tell her and had instead shown her by climbing into the filled bathtub. It was drastic, but he had to wash properly now and then and he did warn her he was going to demonstrate. Even so he'd been surprised by her lack of reaction. She'd simply waited until he was finished, helped him out and gently patted him dry. She stayed with him until his skin had returned to normal and then told him about another lead she'd found.

Katya was the one who suggested he become a freelance journalist. "That way we could work together, I could help keep you dry and you wouldn't have annoying colleagues to worry about."

"You think I can do it?"

"Definitely. You have an uncanny ability to get the truth from people. Anyone you interview confides in you and you get the scoop."

"I suppose that comes from keeping secrets myself. I instinctively know when other people are doing the same thing."

"It could be, yes."

Ethan could perhaps have become both famous and rich if he'd made more frequent use of his talents. A natural shyness coupled with his going off so often in search of all things supernatural meant his scoops were infrequent enough for jealous rivals to almost convince themselves they were no more than lucky flukes.

That suited Ethan just fine. Would Katya want him to be more ambitious though? He asked her that very question when another possible UFO lead had coincided with royal baby news.

"Let's go hunting aliens, shall we?" she said.

It hadn't been much of a story. Someone had graffitied something vaguely rocket shaped onto a bridge using luminous paint. Katya managed to get a good picture in the twilight which made it look mysterious. That earned them a reasonable fee, despite the actual report being short and unexciting. Ethan did come back with big news though; he and Katya were engaged!

For a brief time he'd wondered if she herself could be an alien creature. The cliche 'out of this world' certainly fitted her. She was a perfect match for Ethan who was definitely an oddball and her photographic skill was magical. She dismissed it as down to her excellent camera, but plenty of other photojournalists had even more expensive kit and couldn't capture the results she did.

He trusted her though and when, shortly before the wedding, he'd said she could tell him anything, she'd assured him she was just an ordinary person and he'd half believed her. The human part he accepted, but his Katya was extraordinary.

"This looks promising," she said one day as she scanned through social media. "Someone reckons they've seen scorch marks from a UFO landing when out walking their dog."

"Let's have a look." Ethan joined her at the computer. He knew from experience that dog walkers, or rather their pets, often came across all kinds of things of interest to a journalist.

They contacted the person and were sent a few blurry photographs, a long rambling account of their belief aliens were taking over the world, fears they'd been contaminated by space dust and the vague location of the alleged sighting.

"I'll be happy to show you the exact spot and tell you everything," their lead assured Ethan.

The man met them as arranged, spoke to them at length,

then took them on a long hot walk to a local park. Katya photographed what was clearly nothing more than burnt grass from disposable barbecues.

They explained this to their guide.

"Ah, but that's what they want you to think," he said. "I'm not fooled though, I know extra-terrestrials blend in by seeming like everyone else. I can feel their presence and it's stronger than ever today. They must be coming back tonight."

"Perhaps you're right," Katya humoured him. She and Ethan didn't come back after dark to check though.

"I'd almost rather miss seeing a landing than spend the night listening to him," Katya said. "Besides I think he's mistaken."

"Me too," Ethan agreed. "Let's go home."

Once back, Ethan decided he was so sticky and dusty from the non-adventure that he needed to take a bath.

"That's OK," Katya said. "There's nothing in the diary that I can't handle on my own for the next couple of days." She ran the bath and put towels to warm.

As Ethan relaxed in the water he said, "Do you think we should go over to America and see if we can get into Area 52? I reckon they know the truth about alien life forms there."

Katya watched as her husband's limbs slowly transform into tentacles and said, "I'm almost certain they don't and I'd like to keep it that way."

Ethan thought perhaps he'd misunderstood her last few words. Having his ears turn into gills did affect his hearing. Nothing though would ever change his love for Katya.

13. Jury's Out

Susan tries to distance herself from the prosecutor's words. He's describing to the court how the defendant is alleged to have treated his wife.

As he outlines the case, Susan hears the echoes of a different voice. One which used to say her husband loved her. He didn't want to punish her, but she made it necessary. She tried to make him happy, to make life pleasant for them both, but she never seemed to get it right. Dexter was hurt if he felt she was neglecting him, infuriated if she didn't give him space.

Once, she'd managed to suggest he might be happier without the problems she caused him. He'd reminded her they were together until death did them part. She'd believed that until she learned the truth was far worse.

The doctor informs the court that the victim once attended his surgery for a troubling cough. "She was far more concerned about the disturbance to her husband's sleep than her own poor health," he states. "I examined her and it was clear she'd been beaten. She reluctantly admitted her husband was responsible."

Susan remembers how surprised she'd been to utter the accusation, how shocked that he'd believed her. The doctor had prescribed painkillers as well as the treatment for Susan's cough. He'd also given her leaflets containing information about ways she could seek further help, perhaps even an escape from Dexter. Accepting those had been another mistake.

The defence lawyer takes the stand to cross-examine the doctor. "Is it not the case that she later told you she'd lied about her injuries in order to gain sympathy?"

"She did, but in the presence of her husband and clearly under duress."

The next witness is a friend of Dexter's. Former friend, Susan realises as he talks about Dexter's violent temper. Susan whispers her thanks and sees him direct a puzzled glance in her direction. Surely he hadn't heard her? Even now, Susan can't speak out against her husband.

A former girlfriend of Dexter's also testified about his violent streak. Susan remembered the woman telling her the exact same thing; and that she hadn't believed her until it was too late.

The pathologist gives complicated medical evidence. "The trauma to Susan's Cahill's skull was, without doubt the cause of death," he sums up.

Susan relives the pain and then welcome slump into oblivion as he speaks. This time there's no blood, no body. Nothing to show for her suffering except a tiny flutter of movement from the paperwork closest to her, as she lets out a sigh.

The prosecutor asks, "Was there any evidence of previous injuries?"

"Indeed there was." The pathologist produces photographs and X-rays. "These injuries happened at different times and in neither case is there any record of Mrs Cahill receiving medical treatment."

Susan knows why. What went on within a marriage was private. Advertising any imperfections magnified them. If she pretended everything was fine then sometimes it was. Sometimes he'd been sorry for her pain, grateful for her silence.

The defence provides details of Dexter's good character, charming personality, business achievements and charitable activities. Susan knows this is the truth, but not the whole truth.

All suggestions of Dexter's explosive temper and controlling nature are dismissed as passion to do well, and jealousy from those whose success has not matched his. He asks why anyone would believe Susan's claim her loving husband had hurt her.

"Her later retraction proves her to be a liar. Why would she have stayed if it was true?" he asks the court.

Because of people like his lawyer who saw Dexter's charm and not her covered injuries. And because she too had seen his charm. Because she too had found it difficult to believe he would hurt her; right up until he did it again.

"As has been stated, Susan Cahill died as the result of head injuries. My client does not dispute this, only the cause of them. She was discovered in the middle of the day, when my client was at work. Her body was at the bottom of the stairs. Surely the natural conclusion, and one which there's not a shred of evidence to contradict, is that she fell? Susan Cahill's death is the result of a tragic accident."

He's right. She had fallen. It had been at Dexter's bidding that she'd rushed downstairs, but he hadn't knocked her head against the newel post, or even given her a push to speed her on her way. Perhaps when he'd stepped over her body he'd not realised her spirit had already departed her flesh.

For a moment she'd floated, looking down on the scene. Even then she wasn't free. As Dexter complained about having to make his own breakfast, she'd felt herself dragged into the kitchen with him. When he'd left for work she'd been pulled along behind. It wasn't until his trial that she learned how her body had been discovered and Dexter suspected of killing her.

Susan knew all about the police notifying Dexter of her death and his arrest a few days later, as she'd been with him the whole time. As he was handcuffed and later put in a cell she'd felt herself bound to him. As Dexter told his lies and his lawyer built a defence case, she'd floated above the scene, like a tethered bird. Although uncertain as to exactly how the awful knowledge reached her, Susan knows she will only be free of him once justice is done.

As the judge sums up, Susan feels lighter. The jury will see the truth and pronounce Dexter not guilty. Susan will be free. So will Dexter – to find a new victim. It would be better for him to be locked up for the one time he didn't beat her, and for her to be as shackled to him in death as she was in life, than for him to continue.

As the jury rise, ready to begin deliberations, the ties holding Susan to Dexter momentarily loosen. Seizing her chance, she lunges at the glass of water in front of them both. It hardly moves, but his lawyer stretches out a hand, presumably to steady it.

Again Susan attempts to hurl herself at the glass. It's enough; it falls sending cold water into Dexter's lap.

He leaps up, roaring abuse. Almost immediately he regains control and apologises, blaming the shock and the strain he's been under since the death of his wife.

Susan can't tell from the jurors' faces if that tiny glimpse into his true nature is enough. She has to stay with Dexter as he's taken away to wait. But not for long.

Back in the courtroom the foreman of the jury informs the court that they've reached a unanimous verdict; Dexter Cahill is guilty of murder.

"You can't do this to me!" he screams. He hurls the refilled glass at the jury, swears at the judge, and lands a punch on his lawyer before he's restrained.

Dexter is taken away, but Susan doesn't follow. The jury has made a mistake, yet justice has been achieved. At last she's free of him. She floats away to a place where there's no fear and no pain.

14. Alien Worms

The lunch Aunty served me was just a plate of leaves. Usually I'm not one for salad, but hers tasted amazing. A relief, as I was going to be eating it a lot. I'd got a job near Aunty's house. She'd suggested I stay with her until I was sure it would work out, and I'd had time to find somewhere suitable to rent.

"It would be no trouble, Sasha, and I'd enjoy the company," she'd assured me.

I'd been unemployed for a while, and put on weight sitting at home munching biscuits. As Aunty mostly ate her own produce, accepting her offer would lose me pounds of one kind and save me some of another.

I crunched my way through more tasty, juicy leaves. The salads I'd attempted to make from reduced price lettuce had been a flop. And floppy. "You really know how to make a salad," I complimented her.

"My worms are the real secret."

I shuddered and poked dubiously at my food.

She laughed. "They're not hiding on your plate!"

She explained how her worms broke down organic matter into a form plants could use. "Feed them right and they do the same for us."

I'd feared such a light meal would leave me feeling tired, but at work that afternoon I felt far more energetic than usual.

Dinner that evening was steamed vegetables. Again they tasted wonderful. "It makes so much difference to have really fresh ingredients," I said.

"It's not just the freshness which matters, it's how they're grown," Aunty said, with pride in her voice. Even before I'd eaten any, I'd known Aunty's vegetables were special. She'd won countless prizes in local shows. So many there was jealousy and rumours of cheating amongst a few other gardeners.

Despite the accusations, Aunty still attended the local gardening club. There was a meeting that night, including a talk on alien species. Having nothing better to do, I went along. I learned far more than I needed about Himalayan balsam taking over waterways and New Zealand flatworms eating native populations.

Afterwards there was tea and biscuits. That started off nearly as dull, especially as Aunty disappeared into the kitchen to collect the teabags for her worms. Repeatedly I told people my name, where I was from and explained my interest in gardening. Those enquiries were mostly made by the lady members and, I felt sure, intended to be friendly and welcoming.

Seven members asked me about Aunty's shed and compost heap. Some were polite. Others decidedly pushy. At that stage I'd not gone further than the patio, so even if I'd wanted to I couldn't tell them anything except that Aunty did indeed have a large shed at the far end of the garden. They all seemed to think I was holding something back.

Some people told me about their gardens. A few muttered dire warnings about the threats mentioned in the talk.

One chap told me about a UFO landing in the area.

"Do you think they brought the alien species?" I asked. Almost immediately I regretted my attempt at a joke as he explained, in even more detail than the visiting speaker, what the term alien meant in a gardening context.

Another, much less pleasant, man invaded my personal space to ask if it was true I was there with Rita Norris. Normally I don't talk to men with ill-fitting toupees and mustard coloured cords, but he had me backed into a corner and there seemed little point in denying what I'd freely been saying all evening.

"Yes. I'm her niece."

He hissed, "You'd better watch your step."

I was shocked. Generally I'm considered a nice person, although rather quiet. I'd only been in the village a few hours, I'd refrained for yawning during the talk and not lost my patience under interrogation. What could he have against me?

"I'm sorry if I've offended you…"

Another man pushed into the tiny gap between us. This one had a combover and his trousers were reddish purple. In an angry whisper he said, "The warning is for your own good. We're onto her, so if you're in on it you'll be in trouble too, but if you're not you could be the next victim." His face grew red and tiny bits of spit hit me as he claimed Aunty 'got rid of' potential rivals for vegetable growing trophies.

How could he suggest that about such a lovely, gentle, woman? "I really don't think…" I started to say. Actually I don't know where I'd have gone with that, if the first space invader hadn't interrupted me.

"Major Henderson challenged her about her onions and

has never been seen since."

I decided it was time I left and I wouldn't mind if they never saw me again either.

"A bit dramatic some of them, aren't they?" I said to Aunty as we walked home.

She agreed. "Dutch Elm Disease was terrible of course, but that was before you were born and there's been nothing like it since."

"I meant what they're saying about people, er, going missing."

"Silly fools."

Those last two were more than that, they'd been downright nasty.

Breakfast the next morning was a green smoothie. There was salad for lunch, dinner was vegetable soup. There was a little variation each day, but we ate almost nothing but home grown vegetables. Despite that, I felt better than I could ever remember. My concentration and memory improved. Even better, after eating those delicious, vitamin packed vegetables I no longer wanted cakes and chocolate.

Aunty gave me a small lidded bucket and asked me to bring back the teabags, and any discarded fruit peel from work. "We need to keep those worms fed."

I felt a bit self conscious doing that but obliged as, other than keeping out of the shed, it was the only request Aunty made of me. Actually she was just a touch obsessive over it. Every scrap of paper, toenail clipping and bit of carpet fluff was saved for the worms. She collected hedge trimmings and lawn mowings from her neighbours, and once when a poor pigeon was hit by a passing car she gathered that up too.

I'd assumed Aunty must spend a lot of time gardening, in order to provide all her food, but she told me it wasn't necessary. "The worms do most of the work for me."

I had heard of worms being a gardener's best friend, but hadn't realised quite how helpful they were. Aunty's lived in a special wormery in her shed. No one was allowed to go in there and she rarely did herself.

"It doesn't do to disturb them, especially if they've not been fed," she told me.

That sounded a bit mysterious and I was reminded of the questions I'd been asked in the gardening club. I strolled down the garden, hardly realising I was looking for anything until I saw some military medals poking out of what was presumably the compost heap.

I took them to show Aunty. "You don't want anyone seeing these. They'll think they belonged to Major Henderson."

"Probably do. He was always trying to get into the shed. No matter how often I tell people not to, they still try."

"Should we return them?"

"The sort of person who wears medals to break into a person's shed hoping to find gardening secrets doesn't deserve them back."

I tended to agree, especially if he was anything like his two friends. I guessed the major realised he'd left evidence of his trespass, and embarrassment over that kept him away from the gardening club.

One day an inspector from the Ministry of Agriculture Fisheries and Food came, bristling with ID and other paperwork, and wanting to take soil samples to check for New Zealand flatworms.

"Why would you think there were any here?" Aunty asked.

"We've had reports of sightings."

He couldn't, or wouldn't, say who'd provided this information, but I had a pretty good idea. They were both old and male, had dodgy hair, disgusting trousers, a habit of standing too close to young women, and belonged to the gardening club.

Aunty told the man from the ministry he was wasting his time, but allowed him to do his work. It involved disturbing seedlings, unearthing potatoes and generally damaging the vegetable patch.

When the visiter had gone, Aunty said she too suspected those particular members of the gardening club were behind the visit.

Not long afterwards Aunty received an official looking letter which greatly amused her. She tossed it over to me and I read confirmation there were no alien worms, nor any other cause for concern, in Aunty's garden. The inspector added that he'd noticed 'unusual soil structure' and would like to do more investigations.

"For an expert on alien worms he's exceptionally stupid," Aunty said. "The soil structure is exactly that of worm casts. It's full of vitamins and minerals, so grows healthy vegetables with everything a body needs."

"All due to your worms?"

"Exactly."

"And your compost heap?" I asked. Not being a gardener I didn't know where that came into it, but the gardening club members had certainly thought it important.

"I don't have one. Everything organic goes into the

wormery. The heap is just spoil removed from that and used to feed the garden."

"You must have a lot of worms!"

"Just two. But they're big."

I grinned. "They'd have to be! I want to see this wormery for myself."

"It's in the shed, and what have I told you about going in there?"

"It's not a good idea to disturb the worms, especially if they've not been fed."

"Exactly."

Over the next few days I began to understand how Major Henderson had become so curious he'd trespassed into Aunty's garden and broken into the shed. When I'd ventured down the end of the garden and seen the formidable bolts and padlock, I almost understood why he'd worn his medals to do it. Mostly I was just reluctant to go against Aunty's expressed wish that I stay out, but there also seemed to be something strange about the shed. It seemed to both draw me to it and repel me. Even though I knew where Aunty kept the keys, I didn't go in.

Not that is until the two unpleasant men from the gardening club arrived. They were both worked up into something of a frenzy. That made their awful hair rise and fall, just like President Trump's in a breeze. They demanded to know what Aunty was up to, assured her they already knew, insisted on seeing inside the shed, declared they knew what they'd see, and said she couldn't stop them. All the time they brandished a metal implement.

I think they were disappointed that Aunty stepped aside, saying, "I really don't advise you going into the shed. That's where the worms are and it doesn't do to disturb them."

"You can't stop us."

"I suppose not."

They hesitated for a moment outside the shed, then used their gadget to cut through the padlock. It took both of them some time to do it. One chucked the remains of it aside as the other flung open the door. I'm unclear what happened after that. One second the men were standing outside the shed, the next there was no sign of them. I thought one of them made a noise – an intake of breath as though about to scream or sneeze. Then there was a kind of squelchy, crunchy sound. That went on for quite some time. Then silence.

"It'll be safe now," Aunty said.

It was dark in the shed, except for a faint blue glow. Immediately I realised that the man who'd claimed to see a UFO in the village wasn't a deluded fantasist – he'd seen Aunty's wormery being delivered. That's what the weird box must be, as there was nothing else in the shed.

Aunty stepped toward it and eased open the lid. I peered inside and saw two huge, glowing worms. One coughed and ejected the toupee. I guessed two pairs of disgusting trousers would eventually end up on the spoil heap and Aunty's vegetables would grow better than ever.

15. The Last Taxi Ride

"No problem, we'll have someone there in twenty minutes." The taxi dispatcher replaced the receiver, turned to face the waiting drivers and said, "One for Logan."

"Hey, I'm next," someone complained.

"Take it if you like. Only a short trip and the old dear needs the driver to come and take her cases and help her down the steps…"

"Nah, you're right. It's one for Logan."

He had a reputation for that sort of thing. Some asked for him personally as he'd come to the door and help as needed, not just sit in the car and beep the horn. Logan was happy to help with luggage, willing to talk, or listen, during the journey. On bringing passengers home he'd help with shopping, check they could get in all right and the lights and heating were working.

Colleagues sometimes wondered why he put himself out like that.

"It's not just out the goodness of my heart," Logan replied. "We're offering a service, and…"

"…and trying to make a living! Oldies are slow and given any encouragement take up time you could be earning. Sometimes you realise they're poor and feel bad about taking the money, or even don't in case it means they can't buy food."

Logan knew all about that. He'd had one last week. The old lady visited a friend in hospital and asked if he'd take her home again an hour later. She hadn't understood about waiting times and was horrified over the price.

"If I pay even half that I'll have no money to heat the house until my pension comes through."

Logan had done what he had to on that cold, cold day.

He put the incident out of his mind as the dispatcher gave the address for his latest fare. "She's going to The Willows."

"At this time of night?"

Any trips involving the hospice were sad, but especially those out of hours. The customer had specified she needed help with her cases. That sounded more as though she would be checking in, not visiting someone about to check out as it were, despite the late hour.

Logan was surprised that rather than waiting inside for assistance his fare stood outside a smart and expensive looking house. The lady looked smart and expensive herself, and vaguely familiar. Maybe she used to be someone? She wore rings with large gemstones, had a triple rope of pearls tangled up with her silky scarf, and her luggage was the classy sort.

Logan leapt out to open the door. Her hand, when he took it to help her in, was like ice. As soon as he'd stowed her cases he put the heating on full.

"To Woodside Road, is it?" he checked.

"The Willows. Do you know it?"

He confirmed he knew the way, but didn't comment on the nature of the establishment. He'd let her raise that topic if she wished.

She said nothing for a few minutes, then asked if he'd

mind taking a detour. "There's something I'd like to see for the last time."

"Don't talk like that. You look great." She didn't, not by a long stretch. Not unless you factored in that she was ancient, presumably seriously ill, and you concentrated more on her jewellery and smart clothes than her face – which was what Logan was doing. A little gallantry often meant a bigger tip. It was worth stretching the truth for that.

"I'll take you anywhere you want to go, but I'm afraid a longer route will cost more."

"Oh, that's not an issue."

He supposed it wasn't. If she was going into a hospice then she couldn't have long to live. As he was taking her he guessed she had no family to do that, nor to inherit, so the tax man would get the lot. Such a shame.

As directed Logan took her to the church. She told him she'd married there and her husband's grave was in a peaceful corner of the churchyard.

"Did you want to visit? I don't mind waiting." He really didn't; the meter would be running just the same.

"Thank you, but there's no need. He's not there in the ground and I'll be with him very soon."

The calm way she spoke unsettled him a little. "Straight on to The Willows, then?"

"Yes. That is, unless…"

"Unless?" Logan prompted.

"I was just thinking I'd like to see the sea once more."

"I can take you, but I should warn you it's getting close to midnight."

"I don't mind that, young man. I'm no cinderella and this

taxi won't turn into a pumpkin."

He laughed. "I meant the fair doubles after midnight"

"I don't mind that either."

"Then let's go see the sea!" Logan adjusted the meter to the double rate. There was only twenty minutes to go until midnight and she'd said she didn't mind.

He radioed the dispatcher to say he wouldn't be back as soon as planned, but without giving details. He was toying with the idea of going back to the old lady's house and seeing if there was anything worth taking. No, better not. If he was spotted he'd have no reason to account for his presence there. Safer to stick to grabbing what he could while helping his customers in and out of their homes. He doubted if half of them noticed things had gone. They certainly didn't suspect the nice young man who'd been so kind and warned them to lock up carefully.

Logan took what would have been the scenic route to the beach, had it not been pitch dark. Once they arrived he offered to walk down to the sea with her. Although that would have added quite a lot of time, and therefore money, he was quite pleased she said no. The wind had been bitterly cold when he'd picked her up, it would only be worse on the coast.

He sat through some boring stories about happy times she'd spent there, managing to seem interested by watching the meter clicking over, until she'd finally had enough.

"I'd like you to take me home now," she said.

"Of course. That's if The Willows will still be open?"

"The Willows? Oh no. There's no need for that now. Please just take me back home."

Maybe he'd get inside her house after all. At least that's

what he thought until he arrived at the address he'd collected her from.

"It's just a little further," she said, directing him through empty streets until they arrived at a house he was almost certain he recognised. No, couldn't be. All these old places looked the same in the dark.

He stopped the engine and told her the fare. The amount was so high it seemed easiest to round it up to the nearest ten pounds.

"I have no money."

Her rings and pearls had gone. In place of the expensive coat and silk scarf she wore a padded anorak. Her previously sleek hair was now frizzy and sparse. Logan recognised her as the woman he'd driven to hospital to visit a friend, and the house as the one she'd not been able to heat after paying just half his fare. A fare which had been much higher than she'd expected, because he'd been on the meter as he'd waited, despite the fact he'd parked the taxi and gone for lunch in a nearby cafe. She must have guessed he'd helped himself to whatever he could in order to make up the shortfall and was now trying to get revenge. Well, she had no proof and she wasn't getting away with it.

"You pay, or I take you to the police station," Logan threatened.

"Then let's go see the police!"

The officer was reluctant to leave his warm station for something he felt wasn't a police matter, but Logan insisted. Once the policeman had opened the taxi door, said a few words to the old lady, and briefly touched her hand, he became a lot more interested and called for colleagues to join him.

One removed two bags from the boot. Not classy suitcases, but the stuff he used to carry his fishing gear.

"Hey, those are mine!"

"Thank you for confirming that, sir. And you claim you've been driving this lady around for the last few hours?"

"It's true!"

The bags, when opened, contained all the items Logan had stolen from his passengers, and not yet sold on. Worse though was that the lady was dead and had been for some hours. Oddly the police didn't believe his story that she'd decided to go sightseeing in the dark, nor that he'd done nothing to harm her. In fact they didn't believe a word from him until he said he wanted a lawyer.

16. In The Park At Night

Even before she heard someone burying a body, Kerry wished she hadn't opted to walk home alone from her book group. It took less than ten minutes, was mostly through the tiny park opposite her home, and usually didn't bother her at all.

But usually they'd been discussing a comedy or romance, not a graphic murder mystery and usually her husband walked out to meet her. That night there was a football match on TV and she'd told him not to bother coming out, if he wanted to watch it.

As soon as Kerry turned off the main road she felt uneasy. She was sure she could hear footfalls. Kerry stopped and held her breath. Yes, there was definitely someone behind her.

"Good evening," said the man walking his dog.

"Oh. Evening."

He passed by.

Kerry told herself to get a grip and entered the park with relief; home was almost in sight. Although it was dark, the pale pathways between the trees and beds of shrubs were easy to follow. She was halfway across when she heard a dull thud. There was a short pause and then another thud. It sounded exactly like someone digging a hole to bury a body. That of course was a ridiculous idea, put in her head by the book group discussion.

There was bound to be a perfectly rational explanation. In order to see what was going on Kerry circled around to where her view wasn't so obscured by bushes. In the gloom she could make out what was probably a human figure. They weren't using any kind of light and had their back to Kerry. The thudding had stopped and the person was still.

Kerry thought she could hear laboured breathing. Digging a grave must be tiring. But people didn't commit murder and bury bodies in Little Mallow. Even if they did they wouldn't do it in the middle of the park.

Whoever it was moved again. They definitely had some kind of long handled tool which they struck into the ground, then let out a few choice expressions of annoyance. Maybe they hit a stone or tree root? The voice was that of Kerry's neighbour Leonora. There was absolutely no doubt about that. There was plenty of doubt that she was a murderer, but her husband Gavin was truly awful and Leonora said she was going to have her revenge. In fact she'd said she would get rid of him, and Gavin hadn't been seen for several days…

Kerry hurried home. Maybe on the way she'd think of a perfectly good explanation for what Leonora was up to. If she couldn't then Tom would, or he'd come out and prove she'd just seen a shadow or something. Another few angry sounds from Leonora reached Kerry, who ran.

By the time she got home she'd started to shake. It was a struggle to open the door which she then fell through.

Tom came out from the lounge."You OK?"

"I've just seen Leonora burying Gavin's body!" she gasped.

"Calm down, love." He pulled her into a hug. "Come on now, deep breaths."

She gulped in air as he stroked her back. "I know it sounds mad and I hope I'm wrong."

"Of course you are. Don't I keep telling you about spying on the neighbours and jumping to conclusions?"

He did. In fact he'd done it the previous Sunday.

Kerry had seen her neighbour mowing the lawn, then hanging out washing. Leonora seemed to spend every weekend doing chores, despite having a full-time job and an able bodied husband.

"It's not right!" Kerry had said with feeling.

"Spying on the neighbours?" Tom asked.

"I'm not spying. I just happened to notice how busy she is," Kerry responded from her vantage point at the bedroom window. Admittedly she made a point of noticing what her neighbour was doing, but that was because she worried about her, not because Kerry was nosy. Or least, not entirely.

"And jumping to wild conclusions again?" Tom asked.

"I don't do that!" OK, when Leonora and Gavin moved in she had said it looked as though they were serious drinkers who owned machine guns, but that had been a joke. As soon as Tom suggested those strange looking bags might contain golf clubs and the cardboard boxes were probably some they'd been given to help with packing and no longer full of whisky, she'd realised that must be true.

After Kerry and Tom had turned their mattress and made the bed, Kerry gestured next door. "That husband of hers never lifts a finger," she said.

"You don't know that."

Kerry thought she did know.

"Besides he's away isn't he? Can't cut the grass if you're not at home," Tom reasoned.

Gavin went away for the weekend quite frequently, to watch rugby matches, play golf, attend reunions with old boys from his school and who knows what else. Whether he was home or not, it was always Leonora who did the shopping and other jobs.

Kerry had never seen Gavin at the kitchen sink washing dishes, but she often saw Leonora – hard not to as the neighbours' kitchen looked out into the access passage between the houses. Kerry and Tom had to use it to get to their back garden, and to put the bins out. It wasn't always crockery Leonora washed there either. Gavin apparently had a thing for cashmere socks which he insisted were hand washed.

There was less evidence that Gavin was actively unkind to his wife, not just selfish and lazy, but from a few things Leonora had said, Kerry suspected it.

Not long after the couple first moved in, Kerry had tried to make friends with Leonora.

"There's a film I want to see which is a bit soppy for Tom, fancy coming with me?" she'd suggested.

"Sorry, what with just moving I can't afford to."

At other times she'd tried inviting Leonora in for a coffee or glass of wine after work. "We both get home before our husbands, so we could have an undisturbed girly chat."

Leonora always refused, saying she had to get Gavin's tea, or iron his shirts.

Kerry thought maybe Leonora just didn't like her much and was using a demanding husband as an excuse to socialise. Testing her theory she'd said, "You're very good to him. I hope he appreciates it?"

"Not really, but it's easier to just do what he wants than have a row about it." She then seemed to regret having been so frank, so Kerry had changed the subject. Leonora always seemed happy to talk, just as long as it didn't stop her being at Gavin's beck and call.

Kerry had recently mentioned that Gavin went away quite often. Leonora defended that saying he had a very stressful job and needed time away.

"I can't imagine your job in the doctor's surgery is stress free."

"You're right, but I can't bring it home with me, can I?"

Kerry didn't ask if Gavin often brought home his job of pet food salesman. She did sometimes persuade Leonora to pop in for a coffee when Gavin was away. That's when Kerry learned about his fancy socks, the sales and golf trophies Gavin won, and his wife had to polish, and that Leonora once had a life of her own.

Tom usually left them to chat, but sometimes he'd collect the used cups, offer to make them another drink, or use the vacuum in another room. The last time she'd come round, Leonora, not realising he could hear her, had expressed amazement that Tom helped with housework.

"I don't help Kerry," he said. "Housework isn't her job. Like me she already has one of those, so it's only right we share the tasks at home."

Kerry had been delighted with his response. Even though she probably did do more housework than him, it was the principal which was important.

Once Tom really was out of earshot Leonora said, "My

own marriage is very different from yours."

"I guessed it might be."

"We were happy once, but he's always had more confidence than me and I tended to give in to him a lot. I wanted to be a nurturing wife and somehow that turned into me doing everything for him. Then the few times I did stand up for myself it must have been a shock to him and…" Leonora shrugged.

Maybe she didn't want to admit how bad things were and Kerry wanted to help, not make her uncomfortable. "I can see how that could happen," she said.

"It can't go on," Leonora said almost to herself.

That was only last week, so why was she spending the whole day doing housework? It wasn't as though Gavin was even home. In fact Kerry and Tom hadn't seen him for days.

"I'm going round to see her," Kerry said.

"And offer to do her ironing?"

"Actually I thought I'd take the rest of the wine that's in the fridge."

Leonora had seemed pleased to see her. "Come in, I've got something to tell you."

Over a glass of wine Leonora explained that she'd told Gavin things had to change between them.

"He was furious. Not at what I'd said so much as that I'd had the nerve to say it. I pretty soon realised it wasn't just that I'd got into the habit of going along with whatever he asked of me, but that he'd deliberately been undermining my confidence. He'd tried to make me think that anything I wasn't happy about was my fault and that I imagined his faults. There's a word for it…

"Gaslighting?" Kerry suggested. She'd read about that

kind of emotional abuse and could easily believe Leonora had been victim to it.

"He's not doing it again. I'm getting rid of him."

"Good for you!" Kerry assumed Leonora had filed for divorce. Good. "Make sure you get a good lawyer."

"Don't worry about that, I've hired the best there is and I'll have my revenge!"

Kerry hadn't told Tom the details of her conversation with Leonora. She wasn't sure how much Leonora had meant as a confidence, or if the wine had made her share more than she'd intended. Now she was glad about that. Tom wouldn't have preconceived ideas and would easily be able to think of an innocent reason for what Kerry had witnessed in the park. Except he couldn't. He didn't even believe she'd really seen Leonora.

"Come with me and look then."

"I did say I should have come and met you tonight," he pointed out.

"I know, but you wanted to… Sorry, you're missing the football, but I didn't imagine the whole thing, I'm sure I didn't."

"Don't worry about the footie. You're more important than that. Come on, we'll go and check. Then if there's no one there, and no shallow grave, you'll admit you were mistaken?"

"I will." She'd feel silly, but hoped that would be the case.

It took only a few minutes for them to reach a point were they could hear the thudding and see movement. They retreated for a whispered conference. Tom agreed it did look like someone was doing something out there and that if Kerry thought she'd heard Leonora, then it probably was her.

"But she's not digging a grave?"

Tom couldn't think of a single alternative explanation, nor any innocent reason for her to be doing anything at all in the park at night. "None of that proves she's murdered Gavin though."

Kerry repeated as much as she could remember of the conversation about getting rid of Gavin. "When did you see him last?" she asked Tom.

"His car was there the night after she'd been in for coffee with us, but I didn't actually see him."

"She said she's got a really good lawyer. Why does she need that? They don't have kids so shouldn't it all be straightforward?"

"In theory. Do you think Gavin would make things easy for her?"

"No, definitely not. Maybe it was self defence, not murder."

"Maybe."

"Or an accident after a row?" Kerry suggested.

"That sounds a bit more likely."

"But you don't believe it?"

"I don't know what's going on, but maybe we should call the police?" Tom said.

"I suppose we have to."

"Please don't do that," Leonora said.

Kerry screamed and Tom dropped his phone.

"Sorry, I didn't mean to startle you," Leonora said. "As you were talking about calling the police I thought you must know I was here."

"We did," Tom said, stepping between Leonora and Kerry.

"Please don't call anyone. I haven't really done any harm." She pulled her phone from her pocket, switched on the light and shone it towards where she'd been doing whatever she was doing.

Kerry picked up Tom's phone and did the same. The three of them moved closer, but revealed no sign of a grave, just some scuff marks like those caused by kids playing football.

"I haven't seen Gavin lately," Tom said in what Kerry recognised as his trying to sound casual voice.

"Didn't Kerry say? I've got rid of him."

"She did say something along those lines."

"I've filed for divorce and kicked him out. Of course legally the house is as much his as mine, but once he realised he couldn't bully me into changing my mind he kind of crumbled. I was almost sorry for him."

"You mentioned getting a good lawyer?" Kerry prompted.

"I'll need that. Once he's pulled himself together he'll want the house. A good lawyer will get me enough of a payout to get a flat or something."

"Oh, right. When you said revenge I was expecting something more."

"There is. For someone who isn't very good he's awfully keen on winning golf matches. I'm sure when we moved here and he joined a new club that he lied about his handicap, as he's been bragging about winning. I've signed up for lessons with a pro who says I'm a natural. My plan is to get good enough to beat Gavin. Can you imagine his reaction?"

Kerry could.

"I think I've become a bit obsessed over it, which is why I'm practising out here in the dark. It might be better for my technique if I could use balls, but I'd hate to frighten anyone who was walking across the park at night."

Leonora took a final swing, hitting the ground with a dull thud, which sounded just like someone digging a hole, and sending the last of Gavin's cashmere socks crashing into the undergrowth.

17. Original Period Features

"As you can see the property is bursting with potential."

To Alyson it looked a bit of a mess. "I was really hoping for somewhere I could live in straight away," she told the estate agent.

"Then this is perfect for you. Naturally you'll want to redecorate to put your own stamp on the place."

"I suppose."

"The walls are sound, wiring in good condition…" He rambled on, answering questions she hadn't even thought to ask.

"So, there aren't any problems with the house?" Alyson asked, when she could get a word in.

"There's no chain, so the sale will go through smoothly."

That wasn't what she'd asked. Alyson hated to make a fuss, but she had to be sure the house was suitable. "So, is there…"

"Public transport is very good in this area and of course being so high up means you have wonderful views." He continued with his spiel as though she hadn't spoken, strongly hinting that if she didn't put in an immediate offer she'd lose her chance.

It was just about the only place locally that was within her price range and Alyson did need to find somewhere fast.

Her ex was buying out her share of their former home and had made her so uncomfortable she'd had to leave. Sleeping on her best friend's sofa could only be a very temporary solution.

By the time Shellie arrived, the estate agent was driving away.

"Sorry I'm late… Are those the keys? Oh, Alyson you didn't get pushed into agreeing straight away?"

Alyson shook her head. "He tried, but I had the feeling there was something he wasn't telling me. Eventually I got him to admit there are rumours it's haunted. That doesn't bother me, but somehow it made me feel strong enough to say I wanted more time to think and to look round on my own."

"Well done you! I wish you could be a bit more like that with Steve. He's not treating you at all fairly. Even buying a tiny place like this will leave you with a huge mortgage and he and that woman will…"

Alyson interrupted. "Yeah, I know. Come on, let's have a proper look round."

Without the estate agent bothering her, Alyson saw that although tatty, the house could be made really beautiful. Just for a moment the peeling paper, chipped paint and grimy windows seemed to fade away. In their place Alyson could almost see fresh, bright colour, smooth walls, glossy woodwork, and light streaming in. It would take work, but the result would be worth it.

"I'm going to buy it," Alyson said.

"Are you sure?"

"Yes, for once I know exactly what I want." She took out her phone and offered the estate agent an amount close to the asking price, if the sale was completed within a month. Then she called Steve to say the divorce settlement he'd offered her wasn't good enough. "I'm not signing anything until you make a fair offer."

When she saw Shellie's shocked face, Alyson grinned. "I bet Steve's expression is just like yours."

"I doubt he's so impressed!"

As Shellie drove them back to her place, Alyson started to regret being so decisive. "Steve's going to be furious and the house needs so much doing to it."

"You can kip at mine for as long as you need and if Steve is angry that's not your problem anymore. It'll all be fine."

Shellie was right. Although not exactly gracious about it, Steve did agree to a fairer settlement.

The estate agent was much more pleasant to deal with, especially once her offer was accepted. He told her that a former owner of the house called Elise Montgomery had been some kind of artist who'd become very stubborn in her old age. It was her ghost which was said to haunt the place.

"What does she do?" Alyson asked, more intrigued than alarmed.

"Nothing. None of the people who've owned it since have reported anything actually happening and in any case there are no such things as ghosts. It's just that, for a variety of different reasons, those who've bought the house haven't lived there long and it's been empty now and then. That's why it hasn't been modernised and you were able to buy it for such a reasonable price."

"No one has died there?"

He hesitated. "I can't be certain that Miss Montgomery didn't, but she was in her nineties. Otherwise I'm as sure as I can be that no one else has."

Alyson was as sure as she could be that not only had Elise Montgomery died in the house, but the estate agent was aware of the fact. Alyson would have liked to press him for the truth, but not all of the self confidence she'd briefly felt in the little house had accompanied her to the estate agent's office.

The sale was arranged almost as quickly as had been promised. Despite Shellie's objections, Alyson decided to move in immediately.

"I want to get started on both the decorating and my new life straight away," she explained as the friends carried in Alyson's few possessions and an inflatable mattress.

"But you've got nothing here. No TV, nowhere comfortable to sit, not even a bookshelf or wine rack!"

"Good. That'll make sure I spend all my free time getting the house right."

Shellie sighed. "I can see you're determined."

Alyson needed every bit of that determination. Although the estate agent had been correct that most of the work needed to smarten the place up was superficial, there was a lot of it and Alyson had never done anything like that before. Perhaps Steve had watched some of those DIY programmes on television and she'd subliminally taken in the information as somehow she seemed to know more about the required tasks than she'd realised. She also became rather good at persuading Shellie and any other visitors to assist her stripping old paper and lifting scruffy lino.

Once some of the rooms had been prepared for redecoration, Shellie said, "You could slap a coat of paint on the living room and bedroom walls, bung down some carpet and make Steve give you some furniture from your old place."

"I could, but I'm not going to. The floorboards must be sanded and I'll have rugs so they can be seen. As for the walls, well, it's very important to get everything exactly right."

"More important than not sleeping on the floor?" Shellie asked.

"Yes." She couldn't explain why, but Alyson knew she must tackle each job in order and not move on until the result was perfect.

The old wallpaper in the bathroom was a nightmare to remove. It seemed that previous owners had tried and given up. More than once, judging by the way the edges on some areas were more faded than others. Alyson worked all evening to reveal a tiny square of bare plaster before going to bed exhausted. In the morning she was pleased to see she'd done more than she'd remembered.

The same thing happened the following day, but even so the job was going to take a long time.

Shellie came round the following weekend. "Thought I'd take you shopping for furniture and curtains."

"I'm not ready for that. Grab some paint stripper and help with this woodwork."

"Paint stripper? Can't you hire a machine?"

"No, it needs to be done carefully or I'll spoil the decorative moulding. That has to be preserved."

Shellie looked at the chemicals and tools Alyson was using to clean up the skirting boards. "This will ruin my nails. I'll make us a cup of tea."

"No tea until you've earned it. Get a sponge and soak the next bit of wallpaper. You can wear gloves."

"Slave driver," Shellie said, but she laughed too. "There better be biscuits."

"Nope; really gooey chocolate cake."

Shellie pulled on rubber gloves and began dabbing at the bathroom walls which, despite Alyson's best efforts, still had more papered area than bare plaster. "It'll take forever to get all this off. Why not just cover it over with something?"

"It wouldn't look right. I'm not giving in until it's exactly as it should be!"

"What's got into you?" Shellie asked. "I've never seen you so sure of anything."

"Living here does seem to have made me more confident. That's a good thing, isn't it?"

"I suppose."

"Someone came round a few days ago trying to pressurise me into signing up for really expensive new windows. I not only refused, but reported him for his bullying behaviour."

"Go you! That reminds me, what was the name of your ghost?"

"I suppose you mean Elise Montgomery, but this place can't be haunted. I never feel nervous or lonely here, or as if I'm not wanted. Quite the opposite."

When the walls and woodwork were almost ready, Alyson discovered an old colour chart in a cupboard which she'd previously thought was empty. There was a cross next to an exquisite shade of palest blue, called 'Sky Kiss'. That colour would be perfect for the bathroom. Although she couldn't use it until the windows had been sorted out, she decided to buy the paint immediately.

"I know the chart is quite old, but I wondered if this colour is still available?" she asked the man in the hardware store.

"We've got something just like it," he said. The battered paint tins he eventually produced had faded labels giving the colour as 'Sea Spray'.

"Actually…"

"Found that specially for you," he said.

"Yes, but…"

"I'll give you ten percent off."

"That isn't much of a bargain if it's spoiled or the wrong colour," Alyson pointed out. She suppressed a smile as she remembered Shellie saying she shouldn't be allowed in shops on her own. Sales staff seemed to always make a beeline for Alyson and persuade her to buy all manner of things she neither needed nor wanted.

"Twenty-five percent."

When Alyson made clear she wouldn't take the paint at any price, he said she was stubborn. Steve said much the same, although in stronger terms, when she refused to accept all their old furniture, at his valuation, in lieu of some of the cash he owed her. She hadn't really become stubborn. She was determined and assertive, but not unreasonably so.

When another man came to measure up for her new windows he suggested refurbishing them instead so as not to spoil the character of the house.

"That sounds expensive and time consuming," Alyson said.

"It would be a longer job, but it shouldn't cost any more."

He was right; repaired original windows would look so much better than modern ones. "I'll think about it."

"No rush, but if you agree I will insist each is paid for as it's finished. I ordered replacement windows for this house once before, then the people left before it was done. The house has a reputation for people not staying long."

"I don't intend being scared off by rumours."

"No, I didn't think you would be and that certainly wasn't my intention."

When Alyson told Shellie about the conversation, her friend had grinned. "Oh, and what were his intentions then?"

"Actually he did suggest going for a drink, but I don't think jumping straight into another relationship is a great idea. Don't you think it is good though that he didn't think I was the sort of person to be easily manipulated?"

"About that," Shellie said. "I asked in the library about your friend Elise. It seems she was fairly well known interior designer. Apparently she was very stubborn and had a reputation for never leaving a job unfinished. She'd worked until her nineties, then bought your house."

"And died before she could make it beautiful? That's really sad. I wonder what she had in mind for the place?"

Alyson and Shellie searched in the library and local museum and found old articles written either by Miss Montgomery herself, or about projects she'd overseen. The lady had strongly disliked linoleum or fitted carpets, preferring instead to place good quality rugs over sanded wooden floors. Her favourite shade of paint had been a pale blue known as 'Sky Kiss'. She was always very keen to retain any original features such as decorative mouldings.

"She had great taste," Alyson said after reading Elise's description of her own perfect home.

A little over a year later Alyson had finished redecorating her home, basing her colour schemes and finishing touches on those favoured by Elise Montgomery. The house was of full fresh, bright colour, smooth walls, glossy woodwork, all lit up by light streaming in through the refurbished original windows.

Alyson decided to call her little house at the top of the hill, 'Sky Kiss' and felt sure she would live there happily, and self-confidently, ever after.

18. Life Drawing

"How about you draw a picture of me, Jade love?"

Jade had called into the hospital to visit Gran on her way home from art college and had her sketchpad with her. It would have seemed a natural suggestion except drawing members of her family was something Jade now avoided.

Aged six, Jade told Gran she wanted a Daddy – one who would play games with her and make Mummy laugh.

"Draw a picture of you all together," Gran urged.

It seemed a long time after that when Mum met Lucas. But ten minutes is forever when you're that young. As soon as Lucas was a regular visitor Jade hoped to be bridesmaid when he and Mum married. A wedding hadn't been discussed as far as she knew, but Gran encouraged Jade to draw herself into the role. Jade got to wear a bridesmaid dress very like the one she'd drawn – or how it had been in her head as she moved the pens across the paper at any rate.

Jade was eight by the time she decided a little brother or sister would be nice and drew herself one. She wouldn't have remembered when it was except that the crayons and sketchpad were new – a gift for her birthday. That had been June and her brother was born the following March – slightly over nine months later. Again he looked very like the drawing she'd attempted to create. That wasn't surprising as she'd imagined a miniature version of herself.

Rhys was something of a disappointment once the novelty wore off. He cried a lot and diverted attention from Jade. The family no longer spent an entire day on the beach, or went for long walks along the cliffs as Jade loved to do.

"It's too cold, for a baby," they said. Or, "that would be too long for Rhys to stay out." Jade wished he'd go away and drew a picture of the family without him. That night he'd been really ill and was taken to hospital. His parents went with him and Gran looked after Jade.

In the morning Gran saw the picture. "I'd like it better if Rhys were included and he was well."

"I want that for real," Jade said. She'd been really upset to see him looking so poorly. "I'll draw him getting better." She did so carefully and was still colouring it when they got a call to say he was responding to treatment.

Gran said, "It would probably be best to stick to drawing nice things, Jade love," Gran said. "And to leave your family out of the pictures."

Later she wondered if Gran thought her drawings had some kind of power. In a way perhaps they had. Knowing Jade would accept Mum having a new man in her life, or a new baby, perhaps encouraged those things to happen.

Jade was asked to draw her family at school. Just in case Gran was right, Jade had drawn them all having a celebration. She concentrated on making them look happy and surprised. That night Lucas came home saying he'd bought a scratch-card on a whim and won £1,000. He treated them to a takeaway dinner.

Encouraged, Jade drew pictures of her friends with nice or funny things happening to them. There was no result, but little Rhys laughed at her drawings and to amuse him she drew a picture of him with ragged hair and a giant nose.

That afternoon he managed to tangle himself up in a bramble bush. Mum had to cut some of his hair to free him and a scratch on his nose resulted in a bit of swelling. From then on she'd avoided drawing members of her family.

So, when she was asked to do just that she'd said, "I don't think I should, Gran."

"Please, love. Draw how you'd like to remember me when I'm gone."

Jade finally agreed. Her sketch showed Gran asleep in a deckchair on the beach, with the flower-studded cliffs rising behind her and gulls wheeling overhead.

"That's beautiful, love. Reminds me of my honeymoon." She closed here eyes. "I can hear the waves."

Gran slipped into a coma not long after. Her family didn't know if she could hear them, but the doctors thought it possible, so they said goodbye and kissed her smiling face.

Jade was surprised to inherit a well used sketchbook from Gran – she'd not known she'd drawn. She flipped through, impressed with the way Gran had captured the spirit of people and places, making her certain she'd recognise them if she saw them for real. The last two pages were blank.

She turned back to the final image. It was the same beach her family often visited. Two people, unmistakably her grandparents, looked down from the top of the cliffs. The young woman on the deckchair was clearly Mum. Although the sketch was dated nine months before she was born, Jade had no doubt she was the baby cradled in Mum's arms.

Jade taped her picture of Gran asleep on that same beach onto the first empty page, then filled the last with a drawing of her family no longer grieving, but remembering Gran with love.

19. Perfect Wave

Rick levered his chisel under the edge of the plaster, gave a hefty yet controlled whack with the lump hammer, then stepped to the side as a large piece came away. It landed neatly on the tarpaulin sheet, ready to be lugged down to the skip. He was getting the hang of this at last. He repeated the operation getting the same, pretty near perfect, result each time.

Halfway through he realised the other two had stopped working. Were they watching his technique in admiration? He glanced around to see that although George and Andy were watching him, it was because they'd already stripped the plaster off the rest of the room. Even for such an experienced pair, that was some going!

If they carried on at this rate, they'd be ready for the next stage by Friday morning. As the wood they'd need wasn't scheduled to arrive until Monday lunchtime, Rick might be able to spend a long weekend surfing.

George signalled for Rick to stop work and follow him down the steep stairs and out into the fresh air. All three men pulled off dust masks and wiped their sweaty, grimy faces.

"We're doing great. Deserve an extra tea break, I reckon," George said. He opened his newspaper.

"I'll put the kettle on," Rick volunteered. Might as well

offer, they'd make him do it anyway.

"Reckon we deserve more than that!" Andy said. "That rotten old plaster might be coming down more quickly than the boss estimated, but it's just as much work…"

"Which we're doing in half the time," George finished for him.

"Exactly. So we're working twice as hard. The boss will get extra profit from it, but all we'll get is exhausted. Missus is getting fed up of me coming home and going straight to sleep."

"If I was your missus, I'd be pleased about that!" Rick said, ducking behind a wheelbarrow for safety as Andy aimed a packet of biscuits in his direction.

"Hey!" George said. "Look at this." He showed them a report about how work on a new road had been halted because rare newts had been found on the site. "Those blokes will all be at home on full pay!"

"Or at the beach on full pay," Rick said, thinking longingly of his surfboard and cool salt water.

"Or down the pub on full pay," Andy said.

George looked around the parched garden. "No newts around here, worst luck."

"Wouldn't stop work on the house anyway," Andy pointed out. "We'd need something inside."

"Bats," Rick suggested.

"Yes, you are! How late did you stay last night sorting everything out?"

Rick ignored the first part of that and smiled at the second. The previous day a lorry load of paint and plaster had arrived just as they were about to go home. George had to pick up his son from football practice and Andy was hoping to make it into town in time to collect an anniversary present for his wife.

"I'll deal with it," Rick had offered. Then when he saw their relief added, "And I could come in a bit later tomorrow."

"Fair enough," George had said.

It hadn't taken Rick long to shift the stuff inside and lock it away.

When Rick arrived Wednesday morning, an hour later than usual after catching a few amazing waves, he was surprised to see it all gone from the hallway. For a moment he'd panicked that it had been stolen, but soon saw it had not only been moved out of the way, but was stacked up in groups according to where it would be needed. Someone had worked hard that morning.

"Ghosts!" George said.

"Eh?" Andy queried.

"If this place was haunted, people would come and investigate, right?"

Rick looked back at the building with its collection of sharply pitched roofs, elaborate chimneys and peeling paint. "It does look the sort of place which could be haunted."

"Maybe," Andy agreed. "But I can't see what good that'd do us. They'd just get in the way and say we had too many tea breaks."

"Ghosts would?" Rick asked.

"The investigators, you snoozer! Go on, George."

"Not if the ghosts only appeared because of us stripping off all the old plaster and releasing them… We'd have to stop work and not trap the spirits back inside, wouldn't we?"

"Hmmm, see what you mean… There is something a bit spooky about the place. I mean, look at the way junior here seems almost competent at times."

"Oi!" Rick said. "What are you saying? The house is helping me?"

"All of us, I reckon. That's why work is going so quickly," George said.

"Yeah, now you mention it, there's definitely an atmosphere in that place," Andy said. "And windows are always opening aren't they? That'll be the spirits trying to get free."

'That'll be you and George opening them to try to clear the dust,' Rick thought, but didn't say. He wished he could get free. He'd be straight down the beach and paddling out towards the waves. Judging by what he'd seen that morning and the way the breeze was running, there'd be perfect A-frames out there by now. Maybe even tubes…

He became aware that George and Andy were talking in quiet, serious voices.

"I thought that was you?" Andy said.

"No. If I'd known it was going to rain I would have. Could have kicked myself when I heard it in the morning. Was it you, lad?"

Rick realised they must be talking about the board put up over the gap where an upstairs window had once been. For a moment he considered taking the credit for doing the job and saving them an awful lot of trouble, but resisted. They couldn't really believe he'd come back in his own time and managed to do it himself. He shook his head.

"Then who… or what?"

Rick, having missed part of the conversation, wasn't sure

if they now really did think there were ghostly goings on, or were just pretending to. Either way, George sounded pretty convincing on the phone. Poltergeist, he said it must be, as objects had been moved. He made much of unexpected coldness, omitting the fact they'd only experienced that on the day it rained. Rick's nerves were mentioned, but not the fact he was jumpy because of Andy's likelihood to throw things at him if he thought Rick was being cheeky. He also talked about the age of the house and its likely history; at least one previous owner must have died there surely.

"It could be dangerous," George informed the boss. "I know it sounds a bit fanciful, but I don't want to take the risk, especially as we're ahead of schedule. If you get someone in and reassure us, then we can come back on Monday and still be ahead of the game."

That last bit was true. And what Dave had said earlier about them working twice as hard and the boss making extra money out of the job was also right. Was any of the rest?

Judging from the grin on George's face, that didn't matter. The boss seemed to be doing a lot of talking and saying exactly what George wanted to hear. "Oh definitely… All of us… Ah, see what you mean… Yes, now I come to think of it… I'll email them through tonight… OK, then. Cheers."

"Well?" Dave demanded.

"Us three suspect the place is haunted by a really nice friendly ghost. The boss doesn't want us disturbing him, because he might bring in some publicity and push up the value of this place. Because of that, I'm giving quotes and stuff for the papers and he's going to get in some idiotic experts to try and make contact or some such nonsense. Anyway, we're off work until Monday."

Rick didn't believe in ghosts and wasn't at all sure the other two did either, but he did believe in luck. He was on the receiving end of the good kind. Making the most of it he grabbed his board from the car and raced down the track to the beach.

Things had been going really well for him since they got this job. For one thing the others were much nicer to him. They'd never bullied him exactly, but he'd been the butt of plenty of jokes and known his place as the junior member of the team. Recently they'd started to teach him things, rather than just having him fetch and carry. That had contributed to the speed at which they were working although… Every job had its hiccups and unexpected delays. Every job but this one. OK, there was still work to do, but they'd got through the stages where such issues usually came to light.

Then there was the surfing. Rick had lived in the area all his life, but not known about the tiny beach below this house until the first day working there. He'd looked down from the damaged bedroom window and just knew it would be perfect for surfing. He'd immediately decided to give the sport another try.

Aged fifteen he'd discovered a girl he liked was impressed by surfers and used his birthday money on a board. He'd learned the basics quite quickly, but not as quickly as he'd lost enthusiasm for that girl and transferred his affections to another. The board hadn't often left the family garage since, but it was still there.

Rick had awoken unusually early the next day. It was already hot and the idea of half an hour on the beach before work, and perhaps the same again afterwards to cool down, really appealed. From that morning on it became a regular habit.

The building work had really developed his muscles. He supposed that's why he was so much better on the board these days. All the practice must be a factor too. And the wonderful conditions. On no day since he'd found the beach had the sea been either flat or horribly gnarly. Some days were better than others of course, but the waves had always been surfable.

This morning had been the best yet. And if it hadn't been for his good luck that the lorry turned up when it did the day before, giving him a chance to come in later, he would have missed them. It hadn't taken him long either. The heap of supplies, dumped by the driver and which he'd had to lug inside, had gone down really quickly. Almost as though there'd been two of them on the job…

By then Rick had pulled on his wetsuit and was at the water's edge. He paddled out and immediately caught a fantastic wave. They just got better and better. So did Rick. For the first time ever his cutbacks were smooth and fluid, his attempts at aerials didn't send him tumbling into the foam; Rick and the waves were truly epic. He forgot almost everything but the waves, only returning home when hunger or darkness forced him out of the water.

"That house where you're working was on the local news," his mum said as he ate the food she'd prepared for him. Her words just washed over him.

"Thanks, that was delicious," he said, though he'd eaten so fast he'd barely tasted it.

"Where are you off now?"

"To wax my board, ready for the morning."

"Obsessed you are!" She smiled though as she said it and later brought him a cup of tea and a hunk of her trademark sticky date and walnut cake.

Rick felt totally at peace on the ocean. Free. As though he was at last doing something he'd waited decades for. The feeling didn't quite make sense, but the waves did. Making the most of an opportunity which might never come again was entirely reasonable.

On Monday morning he caught it. THE wave. He didn't try to punt, jump or flip, just rode it all the way in to the shore. It felt like… everything. Afterwards Rick sat on the beach, staring out to sea. He'd experienced something amazing and now it was over. Now what?

He felt himself rise up above the sand and the spray of saltwater breaking on it. Above the high rollers further out. Above the gulls. Up through the clouds.

Rick shook himself. It had been great, but it was just a wave. There'd be lots more. Sure he had to work, but he was young and he got time off. There would be another perfect wave for him one day. In the meantime, he'd be late if he didn't hustle.

As he climbed back up to the house he saw cars and vans parked outside. He'd vaguely noticed vehicles other than his own when he'd parked that morning, but his mind was already down on the beach. George's and Andy's were there of course. So was the Audi his boss drove, one bearing the logo of the local radio station and several more he didn't recognise.

"Rick?" enquired a man holding out what looked like an old fashioned tape recorder.

Rick nodded.

"Can you tell us what you experienced?" This was another man, holding a huge fluffy microphone just above Rick's head.

Rick tried to explain the feeling of freedom and release he'd just experienced. It wasn't easy, already it felt almost as though it had happened to someone else. As his words tailed off, he became aware of an interested crowd gathered around him. His boss and colleagues among them. Of course! They weren't interested in his big wave, but the fictitious ghost.

His boss stepped forward. "As you've heard, the ghost who inhabits this house is friendly and, if you'll forgive the pun, he raises the spirits of all those who step inside."

"That's right," George added. "We've all been happy working here and look forward to finishing the job as soon as you've finished your investigations." He seemed just a little disappointed when told that would be very soon.

In little over an hour, Rick was chipping away at the last of the old plasterboard and helping the others load the skip. As they'd had a late start, and the boss had hung around for a while, they didn't stop for any tea breaks that morning.

At lunchtime, they switched on the radio to listen to the news report about the old house. Most of what Rick had said was cut and the little which remained was a bit of a jumble. Well edited though as it sounded as though he really thought there was a ghost.

"The house has an interesting history," the reporter said. "It's over three hundred years old and was built for an artist who was inspired by the local area. You can see several of his works in our fine museum."

He continued listing all the most notable occupants, including a lady poet, a politician who'd had a complicated love life and a professional surfer who'd once represented Britain at international level and retired to the house to wait for the perfect wave. He'd died there, aged ninety-seven, looking down on to the tiny beach below the house. There was mention of smuggling and shipwrecks way back when and even a possible royal connection.

"Over the last few days a host of experts have conducted a barrage of tests, which they say prove there has been recent supernatural activity, but they were unable to be more specific. Looking at the house and speaking to the men who allegedly awoke this spirit, it's very easy to believe that the place could well be haunted. It seems though that who by will forever remain a mystery."

Not to Rick it didn't. He knew. He, George and Andy had invented the whole thing to give them time to enjoy their son's football match, wedding anniversary and a few sunny days on the beach respectively.

At least, he was almost positive of that.

20. Too Busy To Die

When the car hits me there's a feeling I can only describe as a whoosh and I'm sent flying up into the air. I hardly have time to wonder why there's no pain before I realise my body is still on the ground. Rather than being thrown to safety I'm trapped under the wheels. There's a worried frown on my face. That isn't because I was hit by the car, but the reason for it. My head had been crowded with so many 'to do' things I'd not paid attention to the traffic. Now I can't recall which particular task had been so important that I'd sacrificed my lunch break and everything else.

This is a really inconvenient time to die. We're stocktaking at work, the new lines are coming in and I have staff to train. My daughter Janie needs constant encouragement to do anything more than play with dolls and her big brother treats school more like a social club than preparation for a career. The washing machine is playing up. Victor wants us to sit down and talk, go for a walk or even plan a holiday! There's the garden fence and my mother-in-law's hip and the chamber of commerce's proposal. In short there's just too much to do.

As that thought flashes through my… my what? Not head, that's down there with a paramedic kneeling beside it and getting no response to any of his tests. My soul perhaps. Whatever it is, as I think there's too much to do for me to die, I hear a memory. That of my husband saying 'When isn't there?' It comes to me in a reverberating echo, as though he's said it many times. As indeed he has. Because it's always true. If I'd waited to die until everything was done I'd be immortal and clearly I'm not.

Neither am I alone. I'm still floating, but now there's someone by my side.

"Are you an angel?"

She smiles as though amused. "Aye, so I've been told, hen."

She looks very ordinary. No wings or chiselled cheekbones. I like her, trust her.

"I had so much to do," I tell her. I try to list those unfinished tasks.

Gently she takes my hand and presses one of my fingers to my lips to silence me. She gestures downwards and I see although we're higher now and no longer right above where the car hit me, I still recognise familiar landscapes.

"You've nae left your world, just yet," the angel says, rolling that last r. "You can finish everything you've left undone. Rather you can try to, but you'll nae rest until you've achieved it all, hen."

I mentally read my to 'do list'. Maybe I could visit my children and somehow guide them through life. There are stories of spirits doing that kind of thing. I could count the stock at work, but would I be able to enter the figures onto the computer? And if I could, would they be accepted? No, someone would have to check, so it would be pointless. And I couldn't train the new staff, or get the engineer to fix the washing machine by haunting them. Attempting to finish all that stuff would leave me in the purgatory of always trying and failing. Death would be just like life, except that eventually all those jobs would get done by someone else.

So, I'm not as indispensable as I'd often thought. Not at work anyway. My family can't just transfer in a new manager from a different branch. They'll miss me a great deal but between them they'll get the washing machine fixed and figure out how to use it. They'll buy, cook and eat food, even if not the nutritionally balanced menus I tried so hard to make.

"What's the alternative to trying to finish everything?" I ask the angel.

"Decide what's really important and do that one thing, then you can rest."

My family of course, they're what's important. Not, as I'd previously thought, what I did for them, but simply being with them. Not advising or instructing them, but listening to them.

"That's it, hen. They're here now."

I'm not sure where here is. I can't see anything but light. People seem to come and go. My children are often with me, saying they love me and describing what they've done in their day. It's so much more than I'd been aware of. They don't just play games, but have hopes and fears I'd never made time to listen to.

Victor is always with them. He must have so much more to do now, but he makes time for them – and for me. He comes on his own too, reassuring me Janie and Jacob are being looked after by their gran. "They're looking after her too in a way, by taking her mind off the worry of the operation."

I'd tried to help her by doing little tasks her painful hip

made difficult, and clearing my diary so I could take her in for the replacement I knew she so desperately needed. I'd had no idea she'd been anxious about it.

"Leave the skirting boards and sit down for a minute, Danni love," I recall her saying. I thought she just wanted me to have a rest. Actually I know she did want that, but I'd carried on scrubbing the woodwork and ignoring what I really should have seen.

Victor tells me he loves me. He explains how he's caring for the children and he has those talks I never had time for. My husband doesn't say he misses me now, but that he's felt deprived of my company for a long time. Some of what I hear is words he's saying, but some are things he'd said before – when I was writing shopping lists, ironing sheets and planning rotas.

"He's only twelve, love," he'd said when I fretted that Jacob had no career path in mind, was pushing for him to have a maths tutor, tried to get him to form friendships which would prove to be valuable contacts for later in his life. "Let him be a child a little longer."

"Let's all go for a walk," he'd suggested one Sunday. Actually on a lot of Sundays.

I'd always refused; aerobics in my lunch break was a more efficient way to exercise. So I'd not wasted time watching my kids kick through fallen leaves, searching for the first primrose, chasing rainbows and listening for the cuckoo. Instead I'd got on with tasks so important I can't now recall a single one of them.

Friends and other family members come too. They, and Victor and the children, say how much they love me and how they wish I'd just been able to relax. They'd have helped if I let them. They admit they'd not have done as good a job as me, but would have done their best. They're not talking about now I'm gone, they're talking about before. When I was alive, was physically with them all but too busy to listen, to love, to properly live.

I should have accepted help. Delegated at work. Let my husband be a partner in the true sense of the word. Allowed Janie and Jacob to make the mistakes which are part of childhood – and of growing up. That would have shown my love as much as doing everything. No, more because I'd have spent time with them, not just been a busy blur.

That whoosh feeling I experienced after the car hit me has long gone. I'd felt nothing for a while. Not when the angel spoke to me and not when my loved ones came to me. Nothing physical that is: I'd felt plenty of emotion. Physical sensations are beginning to return.

I feel weird. The nearest I can come to it is Janie's birth. I had a caesarian and afterwards was aware of waking very slowly, not knowing what was real and what wasn't. Actually it's not just the discomfort in my body reminding me of that. There are sounds and smells too. Wherever I am, and I'm certain it isn't heaven, it's exactly like a hospital.

A nurse takes my blood pressure and shines a light into my eyes. When she steps back I think I almost recognise her. Her name badge is partly obscured by the equipment she's been using to check I'm OK, so all I can read is 'Angel'. Probably it says Angela. It could be Angelina or something fancy like that, but she looks too ordinary for such a name. There's nothing at all to suggest she'll have a Scottish accent, but I know she does. I must have heard her speaking to me before.

I have! I've heard her saying I'm in a coma. She's explained what happened to me, and what's being done for me, and how she's certain I'm going to be OK. "But for now, hen, you just rest."

Having no choice, I'd followed her instructions. All those people who'd come and talked to me had really been here.

I open my eyes. Just a fraction, just for a moment, but it's enough to confirm what I'd already guessed. Those people most important to me are still here. Janie is curled up on the bed beside me. Jacob and Victor are in a chair each side of my bed, holding one of my hands. They're also asleep.

I should wake properly, and wake them. Tell them I'm OK. And I will in a minute.

Just for now though I'll rest, just be with them. Nothing is more important than that.

21. Tea Leaves

"I'm starting to see the advantage of commuting," Hayley said as she arrived at work. "Shouldn't be surprised – you said I would!"

"You don't want to take any notice of me," Linda said. She was still upset over yesterday's row with her grandson. He'd called her an interfering old woman. To Hayley, who was even younger than Matty's twenty-four years, she probably seemed even more that way.

"Don't say that. I rely on your readings, in fact… Hey, are you OK?"

"Mmm." Not wanting to dampen her friend's buoyant mood, Linda attempted a smile.

"I have just the thing to cheer you up." Hayley produced a packet of Linda's favourite biscuits. The kind with a layer of caramel under the chocolate. "Make us a cuppa, shall I?"

"Go on then." Linda spoke without her usual enthusiasm. Until yesterday a cup of tea had seemed, if not the answer to all life's problems, at least a step towards finding one. That morning, tea hadn't even felt like a good start to the day.

Hayley made drinks for everyone and distributed them, and the biscuits, around the office. She sat opposite Linda drinking her own, but worked quietly as she sipped. Once she'd finished, she pushed her mug towards Linda.

Linda wasn't in the mood to pretend to read tea leaves. It

was a daft thing to have ever started, but seemed harmless fun at the time. When Hayley was quite new, she'd been sent to buy tea and biscuits and accidentally bought loose leaves. There was a bit of goodnatured teasing when she'd revealed she hadn't known you could buy tea without bags.

In order to deflect attention from the embarrassed girl, Linda offered to read everyone's fortune. She'd predicted a tall, dark handsome stranger for Hayley, a voyage over water for the colleague she'd spotted reading a cruise brochure the previous lunchtime, a big change for the lady who'd been feeling queasy the last few mornings and general happiness and good fortune for everyone else.

Not ten minutes later, a tall, dark-haired man strode into the office. He'd come to do the electrical safety tests, and wore a wedding ring, but as he was fairly good looking everyone decided there was more to his arrival than coincidence. By the following day, when the woman with morning sickness announced her pregnancy and someone else won fifty pounds on a scratch-card, Linda was fully established as a fortune teller.

Linda built on that reputation. She often got things right because as well as knowing the people, she had a fair bit of life experience. If the post boy started coming in more frequently and an office girl blushed when he did, it was easy to 'see' a budding romance in the leaves. She gave hope to people who were down, straightened out silly office disagreements and encouraged people to do things she knew they wanted to try. Sometimes inspiration would strike and she'd just say what came into her head. Those wild guesses contained some truth often enough for Linda to wonder if she really did have a gift.

That was until her grandson visited yesterday. Linda

always did a 'proper' Sunday tea with sandwiches, scones and cake, which Matty almost never missed. At one time he'd brought his girlfriend, Sonia, with him. Linda had been certain they weren't right for each other. She couldn't recall now if she'd thought so before or after she'd read Sonia's leaves the first time, but it was such a strong feeling, and so unlike her to make snap judgements, she was sure it must mean something. She 'saw' fresh starts and new friends for Sonia until Matty stopped bringing her. He still came to tea at Linda's, but no longer confided in her or passed over his empty tea cup. He'd seemed less happy each time she saw him. Something Linda didn't think was entirely due to the distance between them.

A few weeks ago Matty and Sonia split up.

"I'm so sorry, love." Linda had meant it, although only because she could see how unhappy he was.

"Thanks, Gran," he'd said and accepted a hug.

"Shall I read your leaves?" She wanted to reassure him he'd find someone else, someone better.

"There's no point, it's definitely over."

The next two weeks he'd washed up before she could look, but this last Sunday she'd managed to get hold of his cup.

"You'll meet the love of your life on Monday," she'd told him. "But you must act swiftly or risk losing her."

It wasn't what she'd planned to say, but felt right. He was starting a new job in a big firm, and had to get there by train. He'd meet lots of people, including single girls. She'd wanted to encourage him to be open to the possibility, so if he did meet someone suitable he'd smile at her, allow things to develop.

"Show me where it says that," he'd snapped.

"It doesn't say it exactly, it's more of a feeling I get."

"Like the feeling Sonia and I wouldn't work out?"

"Exactly."

"There is no feeling. It's just an excuse to say whatever you want, even be rude to people like you were with Sonia. No wonder she didn't want to stay with me when it was made so obvious she wouldn't be welcome in the family. That's not fortune telling, it's just interfering!"

"Matty, I'm sorry. I just wanted a happy future for you."

"No. You wanted her to go, even though you must have known I'd be miserable without her." He'd left without saying goodbye.

Now Hayley wanted her leaves read and Linda couldn't do it. Matty was right, she was just an interfering old woman. A fraud. She still thought she'd been right about Sonia and Matty not being suited, but she should have got to know the girl properly before forming that conclusion – and even then shouldn't have tried to act on it. Perhaps the seed of doubt she'd sown was what pushed them apart when otherwise the relationship would have lasted? She silently vowed never to interfere in anyone's life again.

"Sorry, Hayley, but I can't see any future for you."

"What's going to happen to me?" she asked in alarm.

"Nothing. What I mean is I can't read your leaves or anyone else's. I never could."

"Of course you can. You've done it loads of times."

"I've only pretended to."

No matter what Linda said, Hayley seemed convinced she'd seen something bad and didn't want to tell her.

That evening Matty came to call.

"I'm sorry, Gran," he said.

Linda tried to apologise too, but Matty didn't give her the chance.

"I shouldn't have got angry and said you were rude to Sonia. You weren't. It's just that when you said I might find, and then lose, the love of my life, I wanted someone to blame for it not working out with her. Now I see it wasn't anyone's fault. We just weren't suited, like you said."

"I'm pleased to hear that. I was worried I'd spoiled things. I've learned my lesson though and won't interfere again."

"But I want you to. On the train this morning there was a girl, just like you said. There was something about her. I smiled and she smiled back, but she got off before I found the nerve to speak to her. Will you read my tea leaves and tell me what to do?"

"Go and put the kettle on." Linda had no intention of reading his leaves, but she would encourage him to look for the girl on Tuesday, and suggest ways he could begin a conversation.

While he was making tea, Linda answered a knock at her door.

It was Hayley. "I'm sorry to bother you at home, but I had to know…"

"Oh dear, you're still worried? Honestly, I didn't see anything bad. Like I told you…"

"You can't really tells fortunes," Hayley interrupted. "OK, but you also said you often get things right because you know people, and you know me quite well, don't you?"

"Well, yes. I suppose I do."

"The thing is, there was this boy on the train this morn…

But that's him!"

Linda introduced them, although it was clear from Matty's expression he'd also recognised Hayley. As he put the tea tray down he whispered, "That's her. Train girl."

"Fetch another cup will you, Matty?"

Linda had finished her tea long before Hayley and Matty. They drank slowly because they were talking so much, beginning with Linda and her readings with each of them recalling funny examples, but moving on to a variety of topics. They laughed a lot and clearly had much in common.

When they'd finished drinking, they glanced at each other and simultaneously pushed their cups towards Linda.

"I've already told you both I don't really have a gift." Was that true? It often seemed she did, maybe not for reading tea leaves, but for bringing people together and making them happy. But she'd vowed never to interfere again…

As she touched the saucers she had a sudden, vivid recollection of a leaflet which had been pushed through her door recently. It was for a new Italian restaurant nearby which promised to be authentic and, perhaps more importantly, romantic.

"Come on, Gran. What do you see?"

"Yes, tell us, Linda. Please."

"Pizza."

"Pizza?" they both queried together.

She fetched the leaflet. "Go on, get out of here the pair of you."

They went, leaving Linda to congratulate herself for not reading their leaves and definitely not interfering in any way.

22. White Rabbits

My big sister Karen was always sketching something. I used to challenge her to draw different things and she always could – if she wanted to. She'd tease me, not in a mean way, but as a kind of game.

"Will you give me a pony?" I'd plead.

She'd grin and set to work. "Like this, Pippa?" she'd ask, showing me a half finished sketch.

"Yes, come on, do the rest!"

Sometimes she did. More often, just as I thought I was getting my way, she'd add stripes or big ears to turn it into a donkey or zebra. What I thought was going to be a cupcake suddenly gained a cone and flake to become a 99. The beautiful shoes I asked her for would be turned into lucky charms on a bracelet, or an illustration in a magazine. I'd pretend to be disappointed, but that's hard to do when you're laughing.

Karen often drew rabbits, which stayed as rabbits when that's what I'd asked for.

"Will you do the back this time, so I can see the fluffy tail?"

"No, that would mean it's going away. You want it to stay, don't you?"

"I suppose."

So she always did the front. "Look, you can see his smile."

Actually I liked that at least as much as I'd have liked the back view, but didn't let on – just as she never admitted to knowing it was true. Karen would often hover her pen as though about to add a tail, then laugh and draw the funny face.

Karen was thirteen when I was born. That's the same age I am now. My arrival must have been as much as a shock to her as it was to my parents; their attention and what little spare money they had would all have been directed her way until then. There must have been things she missed out on as a result, but she never resented having a little sister. I know this for sure as she allowed me to read her diary from that time.

I was always a little less accepting than Karen when I didn't get my own way. Our parents claimed I always wanted what I couldn't have. They had a point. I got all I really needed, and a few small luxuries, but most of the things I wanted they either couldn't afford, or it wasn't practical for me to have.

Once I could write well enough I wanted a diary just like Karen's. I did get that, plus a nice pen to complete it with, but that didn't stop me moaning on almost every page that life wasn't fair. I wasn't allowed a pony, to go to Disneyland, to dye my hair pink…

By then Karen was old enough for boyfriends and I imagine not all her diary entries were suitable for my eyes. Those she did show me were filled with gratitude, humour and love. And of course little sketches.

The rabbits became a joke between us, a not very secret code. That's how she signed cards to me. On my first day at secondary school I found a rabbit sketch in my bag. I'd come across one just before a dentist appointment, or a maths test. When anything important happened she drew a rabbit, just to let me know she was there for me. She'd leave them on a post-it note where she knew I'd find them, or on a piece of paper tucked into my diary.

After her accident I wanted to find some and put them where I could see them, but they were all gone. Who keeps scraps of paper with silly cartoons on? I would have if I'd known. I wanted to believe she'd just popped out somewhere, not that she was lying in hospital surrounded by bleeping machines.

My parents knew we must switch off those machines. I knew it too, but wouldn't agree.

"I want her to get better," I said, knowing I was once again asking for the impossible.

I sat by Karen's bed, tears falling onto her sheet. When I reached for a tissue my hand found a notepad. A rabbit was drawn on it. Not one of my sister's but not a bad effort, though the smile looked sad. Mum must have done it in an attempt to comfort me. That someone else had drawn the rabbit finally showed me that switching the machines off made no difference. Although I could still see her in the hospital bed, in truth my wonderful sister was already gone.

I don't want to turn the page in my diary and see the blank space for the first day of the month. Since I've been old enough to have one, my sister has always found it towards the end of each month and drawn a white rabbit to start off the next. Always.

"Just one more," I whisper. "Please, Karen, just one more rabbit."

I open the diary and see it. A rabbit just like she used to

draw, except… It's the back view, showing a cute fluffy tail. I don't keep my diary locked away, so anyone who comes into the house could theoretically have flipped it open to make a sketch. Either of my parents might do something like that to try to comfort me, but surely they'd have tried to draw the rabbit just as my sister always did?

I could ask them; I'm not going to. I prefer to believe this is Karen's way of saying goodbye – and maybe also of showing she's not far away and that though I can no longer see her, she's still my big sister and looking out for me.

23. Lost And Found

Finding the camera just before my vacation into the wilderness seemed the best luck. I saved the images, intending to trace the owner, but somehow forgot.

Losing my laptop was bad luck.

It being found was worse. The police want to know why it holds photos of eighteen recent murder victims.

24. Magical Lights

They were there again. The two, softly glowing, cherry coloured spots of light seemed to dance and play. There was joy in them, something magical. There had to be. They definitely weren't Chinese lanterns, fireworks or anything else Simon had revealed as the cause of her previous mysterious sightings.

Jennifer had first seen the lights on the evening of her row with Simon. On the face of it the lights were the cause of the argument, but she knew better.

"You OK?" he'd asked.

She hadn't been when she went to stare out the window into the dark. To start with she'd felt as desolate as the patch of waste ground behind her apartment block. Seeing the lights had distracted her from her worries. She described them to Simon.

"Twin UFOs?" he'd teased, not unkindly.

"I don't think they're flying, and they're quite small and, as far as I can tell, they're near the ground. Do you think they could be pixies or sprites?"

"More likely to be kids mucking about with torches," he said.

Her fears ignited into anger. "Why do you always have to suck the joy out of everything? Whatever happens you immediately look for the least appealing alternative."

"Jennifer, that's not true! What I want is to rule out those things."

Now she could see that's what he'd been doing when she'd found the lump. Jennifer had wanted Simon to say it was nothing, just her imagination, a harmless cyst. He'd said it was probably nothing serious, but immediately undone the reassurance by suggesting she go to the doctor and get it checked out as quickly as possible. That had terrified her. She had gone though and, while waiting anxiously for the results, had stared out into the dark and seen the pretty red lights, hoped they were magical.

He'd only done what he always did – teased her about her quest for a mysterious encounter and expressed his scepticism. Whatever she saw, he suggested plausible explanations for her to dismiss.

The night a year or so ago when she'd seen, but not identified, the Chinese lanterns drifting by he'd said, "Maybe it's the Red Arrows travelling back to base?"

"Too slow and far too quiet," she'd pointed out.

"Tail lights reflected in puddles?"

"It hasn't rained for days and they're not going in a straight line."

The more of his ideas she was able to shoot down the more convinced she became she was witnessing something extraordinary. Well, maybe never really convinced, but it gave her hope such a thing was possible. Of one thing she was certain – if Simon ever agreed with her about the aliens, ghosts, spirits or fairies she'd know that really was what she'd seen and have no nagging doubt it was just an optical illusion.

Simon then had done nothing more than be himself.

Maybe he thought she'd be comforted by such normality, but Jennifer hadn't reacted as usual because she was scared. And now she realised he had been too. That understanding came too late. She'd refused his company at the hospital or anywhere else.

The moment it was confirmed her lump really was nothing to worry about she saw he'd been right to push her into getting it checked straight away. Her relief was enormous but without Simon's comment she'd have worried herself stupid for months before doing anything.

He would still be worried. She should at least tell him she was OK – and perhaps admit that he'd been right. When she called his relief showed how much he still cared.

"You weren't right about the lights though," she told him. "They come back every night. Usually a pair, but sometimes more join them. They create intricate patterns then."

"Hmm, I can't think what they can be. I might get a better idea if I saw them myself."

"They're there now. Come over and you'll see for yourself they're something special, something magical."

"I'm on my way."

As she waited for him, Jennifer watched the lights and thought of all the things Simon might claim them to be. It was as though seeing he'd been as scared as her over the lump, and still loved her as much as she loved him, allowed her to see the world as he did.

When Simon arrived she told him, "I think I've worked it out. They're lights on dog's collars, so the owners can see them in the dark."

He glanced out the window. "No Jennifer, you're wrong. There is something special about them." Simon held out his arms, inviting her in for a hug.

She tok a step toward him. "You really believe that?"

"I could be wrong. They could just be dog collar markers. Or you could have been right when you said they were special. Tiny magical creatures with the power to bring us back together. What do you think?"

Jennifer snuggled into his arms. "They're magical, most definitely magical."

Thank you for reading this book. I hope you enjoyed it. If you did, I'd really appreciate it if you could leave a short review on Amazon and/or Goodreads.

To learn more about my writing life, hear about new releases and get a free exclusive ebook, sign up to my newsletter – subscribepage.io/ItLSNa or you can find the link on my website patsycollins.co.uk

More books by Patsy Collins

Novels

Firestarter
Escape To The Country
A Year And A Day
Paint Me A Picture
Leave Nothing But Footprints
Acting Like A Killer

Little Mallow cosy mystery series

Disguised Murder and Community Spirit in Little Mallow
Dependable Friends and Deceitful Neighbours
in Little Mallow
Deadly Words and Innocent Gossip in Little Mallow

Non-fiction

From Story Idea To Reader
(co-written with Rosemary J. Kind)

A Year Of Ideas:
365 sets of writing prompts and exercises

Short story collections

Criminal Intent
Criminal Intent

Over The Garden Fence
Up The Garden Path
Through The Garden Gate
In The Garden Air
Beyond The Garden Wall

No Family Secrets
Can't Choose Your Family
Keep It In The Family
Family Feeling
Happy Families

All That Love Stuff
With Love And Kisses
Lots Of Love
Love Is The Answer

Slightly Spooky Stories I
Slightly Spooky Stories II
Slightly Spooky Stories III
Slightly Spooky Stories V

Just A Job
Perfect Timing
A Way With Words
Dressed To Impress
Coffee & Cake
Not A Drop To Drink
Making A Move
Days To Remember
A Clean Bill Of Health

www.ingramcontent.com/pod-product-compliance
Lightning Source LLC
Chambersburg PA
CBHW070457170726
48291CB00008B/2549